The One to Protect

BOOK TWO

ROSE RIDGE

RANCH

LIZ LOVELOCK

Cover Design by Ben Ellis from Tall Story
Edited by Lauren from Creating Ink
& Lisa Vincent
Proofread by Jenn Lockwood Editing
Formatted by Tami at Integrity Formatting
www.lizlovelockauthor.com

The One to Protect

BOOK TWO

ROSE RIDGE RANCH

LIZ LOVELOCK

Chapter 1

Mirella

WHEN PEOPLE TALK ABOUT THEIR life being turned upside down, or flipped sideways, or doing a complete 360, I've always thought that things must not be as bad as they're making them out to be. Not anymore. My life has been flipped upside down, chopped into tiny, insignificant pieces, and put through a blender. The people who I'd thought cared for and loved me are not who they had seemed to be. They're the kind of people who wear masks to hide their real identities. I couldn't be who they wanted me to be, marry who they wanted me to marry. So, I left. Ran away. Left the world I once knew behind.

They say blood is thicker than water, but in my situation, that's not been the case. My family only saw the dollar signs my future husband would bring to my parents' business, and they didn't care how I felt about it. Now, I'm in a place I never planned to be. After a month, I've decided ranch life isn't my cup of tea. Heck, I don't even drink tea. Gross.

I'm not built for the work that goes on around here. Give me a rooftop party and lots of alcohol, along with some close friends, and I've got myself a good time. I never wanted to be shoveling manure from a stall. I gag at the thought of what awaits me once I leave this room.

I had needed out, away from my family, and the only way I could do that was with the help of Carson, a friend, who arranged for me to stay in Dotty's house. My family and fiancé have the means to hunt me down almost anywhere, but they won't find me here.

I want time to figure out who I am. Who is Mirella? What do I want out of my life? Certainly not to be the high-tea planner and stay-at-home mom—that's what my parents want me to be. After watching my mother be a doting wife, I realized long ago that I didn't want to do that. Or I *won't do it*—that sounds more like me. Not right now, and not with the man they want me to marry.

A boisterous knock at the old, paint-chipped wooden door startles me as I lie in bed with the covers over my head.

"You have some jobs to do around the ranch, girl," Dotty bellows through the closed door.

I roll my eyes. This has been my life for the last month. I've kind of lost track of time, and since my stint with the mustang, where I lost control and found myself being saved from the wild animal and face to face with this tall, dark-haired, and handsome guy, it's like she's punishing me for drawing attention to myself and her. The way she scowled at the neighbor when he dropped me home—wow. If looks could kill, I'd have probably been made to dig the hole and bury the body.

"Okay. Be down shortly," I call, aware I'll move like a turtle, really not wanting to shovel out the horse stalls again, though I know it'll still be waiting for me no matter the time of day.

Knowing Dotty, if I'm not down within the next ten minutes, she'll be back upstairs, and this time, she won't be as polite—not that I'd call her polite. She's rough—tough, even—and takes no crap from anyone, especially the guy next door. Harley, I think his name is. My mind flashes back to when I first arrived, and he saved me from the wild, crazy horse that had a mind of its own. It's a beautiful animal, but riding it probably wasn't the smartest idea I'd ever had—especially since I'd never been on a horse before—and since then, I haven't gone near it.

Flicking the blanket back, I sit upright, my double bed creaking with the movement. I swing my legs over the side. My body aches in places that not even my personal trainer has ever gotten to hurt. I move to the large window. The horse is in the round pen already. I guess Dotty plans to work with the horse today. Perhaps I should learn its name instead of calling it *horse*.

Harley has come to the house a few times, and I've heard him ask about me, but Dotty always tells him to keep his nose out of other people's business. I'm sure she's just doing her job in keeping me safe, but it's so boring. I'm actually surprised he's still coming and checking up on me, because I was so rude to him. My embarrassment was in overdrive that day, and anger was, and always is, my first response. Whenever someone comes to the ranch, I usually just stay out of sight. It's easier than trying to explain who I am. I bought a new phone before leaving, so thankfully, I can still contact those who are my true friends and were on my side when I chose to leave. They helped me pack.

I bend over and slide on my black sneakers. They really aren't black anymore since they're coated in mud and who knows what else. I grab a long-sleeved pink button-up shirt, tug it over my white crop top, and pull my long hair into a messy bun.

With a sigh, I twist the tight, slightly rusted doorknob and head along a small hallway and down the stairs. This house could be one for the antique community. Thankfully, Dotty has updated kitchen appliances, which include a coffee machine. After coming down the stairs, I turn to another small hallway and head through a swinging door where the scent of coffee tickles my senses.

A dark-green travel mug sits on the gray stone counter—the same one she's left out for me every morning, as if she knows my routine. When I glance around, the room is empty. The four-seater wooden table is neat and tidy, as if no one has sat at it today. Curtains and windows are open with the fresh air gently blowing through them. It's a rather open space but not sized for a large group of people.

Dotty prides herself on her home and her animals, but she struggles with the rest of the large property. She's not as young as she once was, like I've seen in her pictures in the hallways. It baffles me how someone her age has managed this place alone. Though there is one wedding photo in the hallway, it doesn't look like she's the bride. I've been too scared to ask her about it because she seems so closed off and doesn't like sharing things about her personal life.

Sometimes, at night, we'll be sitting in the living room, her in her old black leather recliner, her legs curled up under her with a novel in her hand, and I'll be watching something on the small television—at least it's color. There will be a moment of silence, and I'll ask a question, like if she has any kids, and she'll put her book down and stare at me as though she's peering into my soul. Without a word, she'll go back to her book. Clearly, she doesn't like talking about herself. I guess it's fair enough since I am a complete stranger.

Collecting the mug off the counter, I pull the lid off and check the contents. I sniff. *Yep.* Coffee scent hits my senses. Did Dotty make this for me? How sweet.

Pressing the lid back on, I head out the back door and down the few stairs before my shoes crunch on the dirt. Here we go—another day of boring jobs that I absolutely hate. I need something other than my normal, though. My happiness meant nothing to those closest to me, and I couldn't live that life anymore.

Now it's my turn to learn and thrive in a different way.

Chapter 2

Harley

"ARE YOU SURE THIS HORSE was a good choice?" Hudson chuckles as he opens the trailer door.

Another loud thud to the side from the scared, agitated beauty inside has me second-guessing myself. I saw the potential in her eyes the moment I saw her in the auction pen—even if she did try to bite and kick me.

"She's beautiful, isn't she, though?" I admire the chestnut in front of me.

"You do realize that you're no horse whisperer. This one is going to be a handful," Hudson says, adjusting the cap on his head and swiping his arm across his forehead.

I latch the lead onto the bridle and work the horse from the trailer as she fights against me, not wanting to let me close to her. "Believe me, you've all made a great point in letting me know I'm not Delilah. Who was training those two horses before she left with Sebastian?" I snap. These kinds of comments always grate on my nerves.

Hudson raises his hands in defense. "Whoa, ease up. No need to take my head off."

"Why not? Because y'all always think I'm not as good as Delilah." I lead the horse away past the main red barn and to the smaller stables down at the back part of the property near the holiday cabins. It's away from the other animals and any other loud machinery noises that might startle the horse. Last thing I need is her rearing and possibly hurting me.

Hudson catches up with me as I walk away from him and this conversation. "Bro, you know I'm only playing with you. I know you're great at what you do with these animals." He claps me on the shoulder, squeezing. "So, tell me, have you seen this mystery woman again? M?"

I sigh. "Nope. Nothing."

Hudson rubs his chin. "She is a mystery. Maybe that's why you're so drawn to her."

"Maybe, but a part of me just wants to know she's okay. That little horse ride would have scared anyone who doesn't know horses. She's clearly a city girl. I could see that from a mile away." I chuckle. "She wouldn't even talk to me when I walked her back to Dotty's the day of the incident." The horse throws its head back, jerking my arm. I grip the lead rope tighter.

"I'm sure she was just scared. Now, let's get this one settled in. We've got a few boundary fences to fix, thanks to the bull in the back paddock near the old farmhouse," Hudson says as he walks out, leaving me to my thoughts, which are now fully back on my mystery girl, M.

How can I get in contact with her? I really just want to know if she's okay. I can't seem to erase the fear she held in her eyes as Delilah and I helped her. Is she here against her will? Surely Dotty isn't the kind of person who'd keep someone like that.

If I could just see her, talk to her, then possibly, I could finally move on. When someone keeps something from you, it only spurs you on more to dig a little deeper. What is hiding over there?

After I've settled the horse, I pull out my phone and record a video, then send it to Delilah. Her reply is instant.

> **Delilah:** *She is gorgeous! I can't wait to meet her. How is her temperament?*

> **Harley:** *She's a tough one. Been handled wrong for a long time and needs lots of TLC.*

Delilah: *I'll be home in the coming weeks for a little while. I'm happy to help if you want me to. I'm keen to get back for a break and get some work done with a few horses.*

Harley: *It's so weird to hear you say you're keen to come back. It's always been the opposite for you. Not wanting to be here.*

Delilah: *That was before I had Olive. I want her to have the same experiences we had growing up. I wouldn't be as good as I am now with horses if it wasn't for Mom and Dad.*

Harley: *Don't go getting sappy on me. Do you have a date when you'll be home?*

Delilah: *Olive and I will be back in about two weeks. I'll let you or one of the others know closer. I'm getting used to this whole spotlight thing with Sebastian. I think I'm going to die young every time he gets behind the wheel.*

Harley: *He's been doing great. We've all been keeping tabs on his races. Hopefully he can come back soon.*

Delilah: *Yeah, he's planning to come back for about two weeks not long after we get back.*

Harley: *Awesome, see you guys soon. Love ya, sis.*

Delilah: *Right back at you.*

I slip the phone into the back pocket of my worn, faded jeans and sigh. Things will be buzzing when they arrive. Hearing my other sisters and Delilah talk almost every night is great. Olive is their favorite—the first grandchild and niece, so she's quite spoiled for an almost fifteen-month-old. I put my hand out to the horse, and she moves around the pen, agitated. "Come on, girl," I say gently.

The roar of a motor startles the horse. I race outside to grill the person responsible. Hudson grins widely as he drives past in the nosiest truck the property owns. I could kill him. He stops in front of me.

"What the heck, man? You're scaring her." I throw my thumb over my shoulder at the mare bucking and rearing in her stall.

He bites his lip. "Sorry, man. Climb in. Let's get these fences done before dinner. We'll be out here all day by the looks of it. We're going to have to do something about the dang bull." He shakes his head.

I pull the door open and jump in. "Could you have gotten a nosier truck?" I say while buckling my seatbelt. I know what Hudson is like when he's driving.

"This is the one I like to use. It usually has everything we need in it to get the job done effectively." He chuckles, puts the truck in gear, and heads farther down the familiar track.

"Whatever." Our ride becomes a silent one. Ten minutes down the dirt road, we arrive near the fence line. Glancing out the window, I catch a glimpse of long, black hair. I do a double-take, my heart skipping a beat. "Go that way."

"What? Why?" Hudson asks.

"Just do it." I sigh. Is it M? What would she be doing out this far? It's a good distance away from Dotty's ranch. Perhaps I'm dreaming.

As we get closer to the fence line, I look ahead, and sure enough, there she is. "Stop."

Hudson does. My eyes connect with hers, and I'm out of the truck in seconds.

"Hey!" I call and run up to her.

She tugs her pink, long-sleeve top tighter around her small frame. "Hey," she responds shyly, not as mouthy as she was the last time we met.

"I've been trying to catch you. Dotty won't let me near you. You've got yourself a good bodyguard there," I joke, but she doesn't smile.

"For good reason," she snaps, the shyness gone instantly and the sass returning.

I cock a small grin. "Whoa, I only wanted to check and see that you were okay after the mustang incident. You must realize that those horses are normally wild," I offer.

She raises her eyes to meet mine, and the fire within them is scorching. "I'm fine." She sighs, then says, "Thanks for checking."

"How long are you here for?" I probe.

She shrugs. "Don't know, but I better get back before Dotty sees me talking to you." Before I can get another word out, she runs off toward Dotty's.

"A name would be good," I call as she becomes smaller with the distance she covers.

"I guess she's a runner, then," Hudson teases, but I hear the humor in his words.

"Shut up," I grumble. If only she'd give me her name. I can't keep calling her Mystery Girl or M. What's her story?

Chapter 3

Mirella

"STUPID, STUPID," I BERATE MYSELF. The one dang time I decide to try to escape Dotty and all her rules for a short period of time, I run into the one person I shouldn't. I need a moment for myself, and I feel like Dotty is on me all the time about working.

It's like, every which way I go, I've got someone standing there. I'm not used to it.

My family had always left me to my own devices as I grew up. Now, I've got Dotty one way and Harley the other. A part of me really wanted to stay and talk to him, to get to know him, but then I saw he was with someone, and it wasn't the right time.

I scurry back, getting closer to Dotty's home. I've heard and read things about Harley's ranch.

That he and his family work with disabled adults, children, and wounded people, and have a vacation destination. I've seen a number of trail rides departing from their ranch a few times throughout the day. I'm interested in seeing what goes on over there. Dotty wouldn't approve of me going there, though.

One day, I'll stop hiding around here. I mean, it's secluded enough, and my family would never think to find me—a big city girl—out here shoveling horse and cow poop. They wouldn't believe I'd do it, even if there was photo evidence. I'm their princess, born and raised to be perfect in every single way.

I kick rocks as I walk, and one finally gets the better of me as I kick it, and my sneaker goes over the top and causes me to lose my footing. I hit the dirt, extending my arms to save myself. A sharp sting shoots up my arm from my hand. "Ow. Crap."

I right myself and sit on the path, examining my hand, which now has bright-red blood dripping from it. Wrapping it in my shirt, I get up and make my way back to the homestead.

When I glance up from the dirt road, Dotty is waiting for me. "What are you doing all the way out here, girl? Did you forget the jobs you're supposed to do? I mean, if you can't live by my rules here, you can go back to where you came from."

Unwrapping my hand, I say, "I tripped and sliced my hand open."

Dotty's mouth drops open, and she rushes to me. Taking my hand gently in hers, she inspects it.

"Come on, dear. Let's get this cleaned up." Her words are gentle and warm — not like they were a moment ago. Perhaps there's a soft side to her; I just have to peel away the layers of protection she's built around herself.

We walk in silence until we get to the kitchen. "Sit down while I get what I need." She points to the dining table where I do as I'm told. I sigh and shake my head as I take in the gash.

"Do you think it might need stitches?" I ask while gently touching around the area, the bleeding subsiding.

Dotty scoffs. "No, it's nothing I haven't dealt with before." She turns on the faucet, and while something is filling, she brings me over some antiseptic ointment and bandages, enough for a two-inch gash. She brings a small bowl of water and a cloth to the table, settles into the seat beside me, and gets to work cleaning the dirt from my wound.

I hiss. "Dang, that hurts."

"Well, it's not supposed to tickle. Now, how about you tell me what you were doing out there along that track in the first place?" Dotty's piercing gaze meets mine briefly. Her looks can be cold as ice sometimes, and this is one of those moments.

Clearing my throat, I say, "I needed a break, and I didn't see a problem with going for a walk. At least I didn't take the horse this time." I laugh lightly, giving a weak grin.

Dotty stops cleaning and looks up at me, her serious face somewhat scaring me. "Mirella, I don't mind if you want to go for a walk or something, but you need to let me know where you're going and when you might be back, because things like this happen." She gestures to my hand. I nod. "Out here, accidents can happen, and if you get lost, it can become too late to find you. There are lots of properties around here."

"I'm sorry," I say as I hang my head.

"I get that the work you're doing isn't what you signed up for, but it's how we help each other out. I'm not asking for money for you to stay here. I do this because I like to help people in other ways than the normal. Here, there are lots of properties around, and you don't know any of the locals."

Like the Rose Ridge Ranch family. "Do you not like them?" I blurt out. "Your neighbors, I mean."

She's silent for a beat and then says, "It's not that I don't like them. We just haven't gotten along for a long time. It's a story I'd rather not get into with you."

"That explains why you don't talk to the father. But what do you dislike about the children?"

"There are six kids in the family. Hudson, Delilah, and Harley—he's the one you've seen here and who helped with the horse. Then, there's Mabel, Sybil, and Odette. Odette is disabled, which I think played a big part in the ranch becoming the place it is today. Their father runs the show and..." She stops, clears her throat, then continues, "And their mother passed some years ago."

I'm stunned into silence. Anytime I'd asked her previously about the family, she basically hissed at me like a cat and stomped out of the room or away from me. In the last month, this is the most open she's been with me.

"Wow, it's a big family. Do you know them well?"

She busies herself, adding the ointment and then gauze, and as she wraps my wound with a bandage, she says, "I know them well enough."

"Do you not want me to talk to them?"

"You can do what you like, dear, but I thought you wanted to keep a low profile?" She drops the cloth back into the water and scrunches up the trash.

"I will. I'm not about to go shouting from the rooftops that I'm here."

Dotty purses her lips. "Well, you did just fine grabbing young Harley's attention when you took off on the horse."

I rub my hand gently and avert my gaze. "I know that wasn't smart. If I have anything to do with it, I won't be getting back on a horse anytime soon."

"Famous last words, especially if you plan to associate yourself with the Harley kid and his family. They train horses, and I have no doubt he'll get you on one. Though, they'll be much tamer than my black beauty out there. She still needs lots of work." She gives a light tap on my wound. "Anyway, keep that clean, and we'll change it regularly. Wear gloves when doing any yard work so as not to get it infected."

I nod, and she collects the medical supplies and leaves me to my thoughts.

Turning, I glance out the window and take in the vast mountains farther back and the greenery. This isn't a place I ever saw myself, but I'd heard about Dotty's place through a friend who had helped people before. Carson and Dotty have been friends for a while. I suppose there are more people like me in this world, and they need a safe place away from those that cause us pain.

I left a note for my family and closed the door to that part of my life with no plan of ever returning. Now, I'm starting all over again with no direction or idea for what I want to do. I'll probably work here for a few months till I've got some cash saved, and then... I'll leave again. Because I can.

I'm so used to having things planned out for me. My mother was always correcting the way I sat. *"Sit up straight, Mirella. No man wants to marry a woman with bad posture."* It was like a slap in the face. Or the way she would comment on my weight. *"Mirella, you need to go to the gym more and eat less of that sugary garbage."*

So many times, I wanted to jam a donut down her throat. Instead, I continued to eat and enjoy them right in front of her, even if it annoyed her. Those silent scoffs and shakes of her head were enough to drive me to continue to rebel against her and my father. Some girls are built for a life of riches, parties, and arranged marriages, but me? I knew that was my destiny when I was growing up, and as the years went by, it became clear that, yes, I loved parties and riches, but not arranged marriages.

Lyle Tillington is a bigwig in New York. A well-known businessman and bachelor. I'd seen him in the tabloids plenty of times and with a different woman on each occasion. I think we went on three dates over the course of a few weeks, and even in between those, I saw images of him out with other women. I am not going to marry a man who won't respect me. He's a self-centered jerk, and I have no regrets about running away from that.

After rising from the chair, I head back outside and gaze at the trail I just came down. Harley is up there. Dotty said I could talk to them. She seems to be holding something back, which is her decision, but I'd be interested to know more about the boys next door.

"Forget about it today. There will be another time," I mutter to myself and turn toward the chicken coop. Time to get back to work and stop thinking about a guy who I'll most likely leave behind.

Chapter 4

Mirella

AFTER A FITFUL NIGHT'S SLEEP, I wake with a throbbing hand. Who knew a cut could cause this kind of pain? It's still dark behind the curtains in my room. I rise from my bed, and it squeaks as I move. I slip on my sneakers and a light coat, since mornings before the sun are chilly, and I head downstairs.

This is a first—no Dotty awake before me. I take some pain relievers and head out the back door. Needing to clear my head, I walk down the track I began to explore yesterday. There's no one around. The sound of the early morning birds is a song to my fractured heart. No one really wants to believe their family members are douchebags, but sometimes we don't have any choice in the matter.

The dirt crunches under my shoe, and a shiver runs down my spine. I make my way to the old house that sits on the opposite side of the fence, on Harley's side. It's drawn my attention since the day I first laid eyes on it. I love old things, things with good history, and this house looks to have a thousand stories within its walls.

The outside has faded to a light blue. Paint is missing in places, and some windows are even cracked. Aside from that, it still looks structurally sound and almost loveable. It sits peacefully on the ground, holding onto its secrets. My heart races as I slip through the fence and make my way over to it.

Hesitantly, I step onto the porch. I release a breath, thankful my foot didn't go right through the wooden decking. I'm not sure how long this place has been here, but it's clear that it's been a while. There's some long grass around the edges of the building. I'm guessing the cattle don't eat right to the corners.

My body vibrates with excitement as I grip the rusted knob and twist. I suck in a sharp breath when the door opens slightly. It takes a bit of effort to push it all the way open. I have to use my body weight. Again, I'm sighing with relief when I haven't broken anything, and the house is still intact.

Inside steals my breath. White sheets cover old furniture. Dust has settled on top of them. It's a small area that leads into a tiny kitchen. Thankfully, there are no dirty dishes or anything like that kind of surprise, just a simple table with four chairs. Off the kitchen, there's a small room. It looks to be possibly an old bedroom. I make my way inside, the dust tickling my nose, and I resist the urge to sneeze. This place is amazing. My history-buff heart is loving this. It must have been the original home that came with the land. That's the only explanation for it. Especially since it's sitting out here, empty and covered with layer upon layer of dust.

The bedroom has faded-yellow curtains still hanging, a little worse for wear, though. I make my way over to the old metal-frame bed with another sheet covering the mattress, and I crouch down to look underneath it.

There, against the wall, it looks like a pile of dust, but it's not. It appears to be a book of some kind. Lying on the floor, I slide under the bed, a sneeze escaping me. The dust becomes worse as I move around. My fingers grab the book under the dusty bed, and I slide back out.

Getting up, I place the book on the bed and clean myself off while coughing up a lung. "Gee, that's bad."

Taking the book, I fan through the pages and notice handwriting, but the sound of a horse close by startles me. Tucking the book in my arms, I make a quick exit, shutting the stiff door behind me.

"You do realize that this is called trespassing," a deep, low voice startles me. I drop the notebook and turn.

Harley stands there with a warm grin across his face as he holds onto the reins of a horse that stands beside him, head down, munching away on the grass.

"Oh, um, yeah, sorry." Bending over, I pick up the book and hug it to my chest, hoping he doesn't want me to hand it over.

"Oh, I don't mind, but other people around these places might shoot before asking questions." His gaze travels up and down my body. "Have you been rolling on the floor in there? Because you look like you collected a quarter of what's in that place." He chuckles and gestures to the house behind me.

I giggle nervously. I sound somewhat stupid, even to myself. "Something like that maybe." I make a move to step down from the porch and head back toward the fence dividing the property.

"It's the first homestead for the property," he says.

I pause, wanting to hear what else he knows.

He continues, and I turn back to him. "Our family has owned this piece of land for a long time. When the family grew too big, it became clear that this little place wasn't going to cut it anymore."

I take in his fresh morning appearance. He's got damp hair, and he's bright-eyed, not tired-looking at all. Yet, I'm sure I look like a hot mess who rolled in the dust. What a great contrast.

Clearing my throat, I say, "Why not use it as a granny flat or something? Why leave it to basically go to waste?"

Harley runs his fingers through his hair and then down his face before his glassy eyes meet mine. "It was a place my mother would come to just have a moment of peace. Since she passed away, it's been empty." His words catch in his throat, and it's his turn now to clear it. The emotion in his eyes breaks my heart.

I take a hesitant step toward him and wrap my fingers around his arm. "I'm so sorry for your loss. I can't imagine how it must feel to lose a parent. Oh, well, I could, but not in the way you lost your mom." Oops. I think I gave too much away.

Harley swipes away a small tear and cocks an eyebrow. "What do you mean?" Those dark-chocolate eyes bore into mine. As the sun rises, its light touches the foggy areas and clears those clouds that surround us.

I remove my hand from his arm and wave away his question. "Oh, nothing. Sorry. I shouldn't have said anything."

He nods, but it's clear that he wants to ask more questions. "So, are you allowed to talk to me yet? Has Dotty given her seal of approval?"

"What do you mean?"

"Well, it's clear that she doesn't want me near you or to even talk to you, and yet, here you are, talking to me. You even touched my arm." His mouth forms a mocking *O* shape.

I shake my head, grinning. "Ladies and gentlemen, it seems we have a comedian in our midst."

"Oh, ouch." His hand grips his black tee.

"How did you know I was out here, by the way?" I ask.

Harley takes my arm gently and leads me out to the fence line. Up the way a little farther, there's a long post. "There's a camera attached to that."

Embarrassment washes over me. "I feel stupid. Sorry. I just find old houses and things that hold some history fascinating, and today... well, it caught my curiosity, and I didn't think I'd be under video surveillance."

Harley rubs the stubble on his chin. "Well, I think I should take you to one of my favorite spots. I can't say it's full of history, but I think it's a place you would enjoy. Actually, I'm not entirely sure what you would enjoy, being a city girl and all," he teases with a wicked half grin and warm gaze.

My heart thunders away in my chest. The swirling of butterflies in my stomach has gone into overdrive. Lyle never gave me these kinds of feelings. "How can you tell I'm a city girl?"

Harley glances down at my sneakers, then back up to my face. The weight of his stare is so heavy that I shuffle on my feet. "Well, first, a country girl has at least one pair of boots. But really, I knew it from the first day I met you. You're not a rider. Clear city-girl vibe coming from you. Where are you from?"

Chewing my lip, I contemplate telling him the truth or not and decide I don't want to live my life with lies hanging over me. Especially if I'm going to start fresh. "I'm from New York."

"Oh, a *big*-city girl. That really does explain so much. How is it you find yourself out here in the woods?" he probes, throwing his arms up and gesturing around us.

"Let's just say that things weren't working out where I was, and so I needed a break." I grip the book tighter to my chest, frightened that my sweaty hands might make me drop it, and then he'll notice it. For all he knows, it could be my journal or notebook.

"How did you find yourself at Dotty's? She's not the most welcoming person," he says and leans against the wooden fencing. With that cowboy swagger, he looks as though he could be in a photoshoot for a magazine.

"A friend helped me." It's all I offer. "Yes, she can be a hard nut to crack, and she doesn't give anything away on a personal level. I've asked about photos, and she walks away from me or simply ignores me. She's good at the latter. How long have you known her?"

Harley scratches his cheek before answering—another sexy model move. "If I'm being honest, I've never really had much to do with her. She and my father have never seen eye to eye or even had a civil conversation with each other that I've known about. Hudson, my older brother, and Delilah, my sister, have asked Dad about Dotty, and his answer is always the same: he wants nothing to do with her." Harley shrugs.

"Hmm... that's interesting. Kinda makes me want to find out what the story is there." I laugh nervously. We stop and stare at each other. I soak in his masculine appearance. His olive complexion, bulging biceps, and that perfect jawline sings the song for every woman—well, at least me. There's something about him I can't seem to put my finger on. Am I allowed to let myself see what, if anything, could come from this possible friendship?

Chapter 5

Harley

HER EYES ROAM OVER ME as I stand here, and I can't help but drink her in like a cold beer on a warm day. She is beautiful. Her dark hair is in a messy bun, but strands fall over her face.

"So, there's something I want to know," I say as she shakes her head slightly.

"What's that?"

I clear my throat. "What's your name? I mean, I could keep calling you M or Mystery Girl, but I think your name might be better."

She laughs and sends a ripple of joy into the mountains. It brings a smile to my face. "Well, I guess I better tell you since I know your name. It's Mirella."

I stick my hand out. "Nice to meet you, Mirella. I'm Harley."

Mirella takes my hand. "Nice to *officially* meet you." We release our hands, but her warmth is still present on my palm.

The sun becomes a little brighter and warmer. Time has gotten away from me. "I better get back before my dad thinks I'm slacking off," I say.

She shuffles on her feet. "We wouldn't want that now, would we? I'm sure Dotty will think I'm still in bed. You know, me being a city girl and all," she jokes.

There's something about her — and I need to see her again. "Now that we've officially met, is there a way I could contact you? We have bonfires at the ranch often with workers and guests. I'd like to invite you to come to one — if you're interested."

"I'd like that. I think it's time I got out and made some friends in the area. Do you have your phone on you? I'll give you my number."

Shaking my head, I say, "No, sorry. Not on me. I was momentarily distracted by seeing you out here and left it sitting on my bedside table." I smirk and notice her gaze shift to Chester. "You know, if you like, I could teach you how to ride."

Shaking her head. "Don't expect me to ever get back on one of them again. I've done my time."

"Oh, come on. Let me teach you the correct way to ride, and it won't be as scary. I'll put you on the mellowest horse we own. She gets used for therapy with children. Trust me, she wouldn't hurt a fly."

Mirella lifts an eyebrow. "I highly doubt that. She'd probably stomp on it if she could and if it was buzzing around her, annoying her."

I laugh. The way she sounds so serious, it makes my lips twitch. One day I might get her on a horse, depending on how long she plans to stick around here.

Silence falls between us, but the world around is waking as the birds sing their morning songs and the sun hits the trees, lighting everything up.

"How about I meet you out here tomorrow morning, and we can swap numbers then?" she asks, her words pulling me back. I shake my head as she returns to the original line of questioning.

"Mornings are usually my busiest time of day with getting things ready for the appointments and guests. It was the security camera alert that got me out here." I wink, and a slight pink brightens her cheeks.

"Sorry again about that. What about the afternoon?" She almost sounds hopeful.

"How about late afternoon, like four or four-thirty?" I offer.

Mirella nods. "Okay, that sounds good. I better get back, or Dotty won't be happy. I'll see you tomorrow." She moves past me and slips through the fence. With one last look over her shoulder, she heads back toward Dotty's homestead.

I can't help but wonder why she's here. Why is she staying with Dotty? How does Dotty fit into all of this? I wish Dad would tell us what the deal is there. I mean, we're neighbors, and Dad has always helped his neighbors out— except when it comes to her. I'm going to have to ask him the hard questions.

Chester grazes a little from where I'm standing, his chestnut coat glistening under the rays of sun. "All right, buddy. Time to head back."

Grabbing his reins, I take a moment and stare at the house—Mom's house, or the cottage, as she liked to refer to it. I haven't been in there in years. An overwhelming swarm of emotions slam into me. Mom should be here, enjoying her kids, her granddaughter, Olive, and just her life in general. Sometimes, life isn't fair.

After climbing back into the saddle, I give Chester a light press with my heels and a click of my tongue, and he begins to move slowly. I take my time heading back, processing the events of this morning. Being woken by my security alarm wasn't what I'd expected, and when I saw it was Mirella on the camera, I moved more quickly than I had in a long time.

I can't help but wonder why she's suddenly okay to talk to me. She was quite standoffish when we had our first encounter. I'm glad I got to talk to her, though. It was great to actually speak with her and see that the wild mustang ride hadn't hurt her.

I give Chester a harder nudge. He gathers his speed, and before we know it, the homestead and barn have come back into view. I pull Chester to a halt at the stalls where I'm keeping the horse I'm training. Thankfully, she's settled down a little now.

Tying Chester to the barn, I step inside and move toward the new horse's stall. She throws her head around a little. I go to the closet and pull out some treats to hopefully persuade her that I'm not one of the bad guys who hurt her at her previous home.

"It's okay, girl," I coo as I unclick the latch and step inside.

She moves to the far side of the pen and stomps her hooves. A warning. I wish all women came with warnings like this sometimes. Though, I'd never say that out loud. Having five sisters has taught me better than that.

"I won't hurt you. You're a beautiful girl," I continue, though the horse's ears remain turned back against her head—a sign she's not ready to let me near her.

Slowly, I move closer, step by step, pausing after each one. I outstretch my hand and place it in front of her nose so she becomes familiar with my scent. I don't want to spook her.

One of her legs kicks out at me but misses, and I try not to flinch. It wouldn't be the first time, nor will it be the last time I've been kicked.

With ease, I place my hand on the top of her head and give her a gentle pat down her nose. Her body twitches and trembles. "It's okay. I won't hurt you. You're safe here with me. I won't hurt you," I continue to assure her.

I do this for the next thirty minutes, and by the end, she's settled a little more. She's not going to feel safe with me right away, but in time, she will. I've not had a horse I couldn't help before, and if I struggle, Dee has always found a way around the issue. The horse whisperer, she is.

"Looks like you've made some progress," a soft voice startles me.

I turn to find Mabel leaning against the gate. Thankfully, she's not like Hudson and doesn't startle the animals with a loud car.

I smile a greeting. "Hey, yeah, she's doing good. It's going to take some time, but once she's settled, she'll be unstoppable. Either ready to sell or use around the ranch."

"That's good. Where did you run off to this morning?"

Giving the horse one last little scratch, I exit the stall, locking it behind me. I turn to Mabel. "What are you talking about?"

"Do you forget that our rooms are beside each other, and the walls in the house are paper thin?" Her hazel eyes burn into mine, full of questions.

I sigh. "The boundary security alarm went off, so I went to inspect to make sure the bull wasn't messing things up again. Hudson and I only cleaned up one mess yesterday."

"Riiight," she says, the single word full of skepticism. "You could have easily looked at the camera, which I'm sure you would have done. Who was out there? Do we need to let Dad know?" she pushes. Gee, she's a nosey one.

"No, Dad doesn't need to know. It was the girl from Dotty's. She was at Mom's cottage. Was just curious about it." I rush the last bit out since Mabel's mouth dropped open at the mention of Mom's cottage. Everyone is very protective of it, yet no one wants to ever go out and maintain it. Too many painful memories. The door was shut, and that was that—kind of like the library.

"What did she do?" Mabel asked, almost breathless.

"Nothing. She went in and walked out—that was it. It's not like she was setting fire to the place or anything," I joke.

I head out the door and untie Chester. Mabel's hand on mine makes me pause. "I wasn't suggesting she'd do that. I was curious, that's all. I mean, have you gone inside since Mom passed?" She chokes on the last word, the pain still raw, even though it was ten years ago. Every day, Mom's missed. The heart of the ranch was taken too soon.

"No, I think I worry about the memories that will hit me when I walk in there. Seeing Mirella walk out today, I almost called out for Mom. That would have been weird, but still." I give a small chuckle.

"So, her name is Mirella?" Mabel's eyes go wide as she flicks a bit of her light-brown hair from her face.

"Uh, yep. She finally gave me her name. It might have been because I caught her red-handed, I don't know, but we're going to meet up again out there at the cottage tomorrow afternoon." I almost don't want to tell Mabel, but I know she's one who can keep a secret. Her and Dee can. The others? Not so much.

"That's cool. At least the cottage might stop collecting dust and be used once more," Mabel says.

I tug on Chester's reins and start leading him back up the road to the big barn, Mabel walking beside me. "Whoa, hold on. Who said I was going to go inside?"

Mabel gives me a bewildered glance. "Why wouldn't you? Or are you just planning to sit on the grass outside?"

I nod. "Yes, no, that was part of my plan. Mabel, you have to know how we all feel about that place."

"I get that, and it was the same for the library, which is now open thanks to Delilah. Maybe it's up to you to bring life back into the cottage, house, whatever you want to call it. Mom would love that." Mabel crosses her arms over her chest, hugging herself.

We walk the rest of the way in silence. When I turn to head into the barn, she says, "Don't be afraid of the memories, no matter how painful they may seem."

"Thanks, Mabs. Are you heading into town today?"

"Yep. Do you need anything?"

"Hmm… maybe some sweets or something to impress the girl next door."

She laughs. "You got it, bro."

We go our separate ways, and her words still cause a slight rattle within me. *'Don't be afraid of the memories.'* My memories of Mom are great, except for the one where I found her collapsed in the cottage — the same cottage Mirella walked out of today.

Chapter 6

Mirella

As I ARRIVE BACK AT the house, Dotty steps onto the back patio, a smile—yes, a smile—on her face. Did I step back into another dimension when I came out of that cottage today? First Harley was there, and now Dotty is greeting me with an uncharacteristic smile.

"Is something going on?" I ask hesitantly as I stop at the bottom of the steps, Dotty glancing down at me.

"No, dear. I'm just happy and shocked to see you up and about this early and also thankful I don't have to wake you up this morning. Where have you been?" She takes a sip of her steaming cup of coffee, and my mouth waters at the thought of my own cup.

"I didn't sleep very well, and I woke up and couldn't go back to sleep, so I went for a walk." My vague answer isn't much, but she shrugs and nods. I wonder what she'd think if I told her where I was and who I was with. Even if she did say she didn't mind, perhaps, deep down, it might bother her.

"Okay, well, get yourself ready for the day. We have people coming to look at the sheep I'm selling." She steps down and heads out to the barn and the pens where the sheep are waiting to be sold. Living on a ranch is nothing like I'd expected. You're always busy. I grew up in a lifestyle the complete opposite to this, and it's one I have no desire to go back to. Hard work or not, I won't ever return to my previous life. I'll stay hidden and out of sight until the time is right. So long as that life never finds its way out here, I'm safe.

I pull the book out from the back of my jeans. I didn't want questions from Dotty about it. Heading inside, the scent of coffee hits me, and I quickly make myself a travel mug with some sweetener and a little cream. I go to my room, sit on my bed, and finally flick open the book's first page and discover it's not just any notebook — it's a journal or diary of some kind. Handwritten words cover these pages like they're telling me a story from way back in the day. Yellowing on the page edges is a sure sign of how old this is.

My heart races as I flick through the pages, not really reading it, but I stumble across the name Olive. In fact, the author of the journal signs off with Olive. Who could that be? Does this belong to Harley's mother? A gnawing feeling irritates my stomach. I should tell Harley, but it's not my place. I do wonder if it is Harley's mother, though.

Going back to the start, I take a deep breath. "Wow," I breathe. The excitement bubbles through me. My fingers glide over the yellowed pages and stop back at the first entry.

This isn't how it is supposed to happen. I'm supposed to marry and then have children, not the other way around. My mom and dad are going to kill me. I needed to tell someone, so I told Dotty. She's always had my back and never judges me.

I love Ryan, and he loves me. Surely, he'll make things right, and we can get married. After that barn dance and the way he made me feel like the only woman who held his heart... I knew from then on that we were meant to be together.

Dotty didn't judge me. Instead, she cried and hugged me as all good sisters would do. I made her promise not to tell Mom and Dad until I was ready. They've been wanting me to marry the boy next door, but I can't. My heart belongs to another. Don't get me wrong—William is a great man but not the man for me. Oh, how Mother is going to kill me, and Father may kill Ryan.

One night has ruined everything. I need to talk to Ryan. We're going to meet up at the old Reily homestead along the fence line later tonight. He's been working on their ranch, helping with cattle and things. That's how we met—he was fixing the fences, and I happened to be riding past with William. William was quick to become a part of the conversation as if trying to interject himself between me and Ryan. From there, things blossomed. I only have eyes for Ryan.

I hope Ryan is happy when I tell him the news. I'm not sure I could terminate a baby. I don't have it within me. It'll all work out. It has to.

Until next time,

Olive

I sit there, my mouth hanging wide open, my body trembling. This diary belonged to Dotty's sister. She was pregnant. "Oh, my goodness." The want to keep reading is strong, but I know that if I don't go do what needs to be done, Dotty will be back up here and rousing on me. I don't want to be the reason for her smile to be gone.

Could that be Olive in the pictures in the hallway downstairs? As I get up, the book falls to the ground, and some photos slip out of the side. Picking them and the book back up, I inspect the black-and-white photos. Two young women. Sisters. Their smiles wide and bright. On the back, one photo has writing: *Me and Dotty.*

I look at another photo. There's one of a lady I'm guessing is Olive and a well-kept young man. He looks identical to Harley's brother—the one I saw briefly yesterday. Wow. I have stumbled across something that's possibly been buried for who knows how long. Did Dotty's sister and the man next door have an affair? What am I going to do about this?"

Then, I take a glance at the final photo, and it's of Olive and a different man. He has similarities in his chin and hair that remind me of Harley. Is this Harley's dad? I'm so confused.

I pick up my phone and message a friend I've kept in contact with since leaving and changing my number. Casey. She's like the sister I never had. She's always had my back, and the day I came to her and told her about leaving, she helped me pack and leave. That was how I knew she was one person I could trust.

> **Mirella:** Casey, you're not going to believe what I've found. It's mind-blowing.

> **Casey:** Wow, it's so good to finally hear from you. It's been too long since our last message. I've been so worried. How dare you not contact me sooner? Your family has been ringing me constantly to find out if I know where you are. They are relentless.

> **Mirella:** I'm sorry. Things have gotten away from me here. I'm always busy. It's a good thing I never told you where I was going. You're technically not lying to them. So don't worry.

> **Casey:** Even if I knew, I wouldn't tell them, because there's no way I would have let you marry that man. He's been off with a different woman almost every other day. That's not someone who is ready to settle

down and get married. You would have been divorced within six months. He's a jerk. He even tried to hit on me after you first left, and I kicked him out of my apartment. He, of course, left with his tail between his legs. I told him he didn't deserve you and would never be good enough for you.

Anger rushes through me as I read her message. How could my parents want me to have this man in my life? I mean, it's not like they are blind. Surely, they have to see him for the kind of man he really is.

Mirella: *I'm glad I'm no longer there to deal with them or him. If they ask, you can let them know I'm okay and that I'm not planning to come home anytime soon, even if I find it hard where I am. Home will never be a place I feel safe, especially if my parents keep trying to marry me off to the worst people in the world.*

Casey: *I've got your back. So, tell me, what did you find? And tell me what's been going on with you, other than you being busy. I need more details or even a picture. It's not like I could find you from a photo.*

Mirella: *I found a journal that looks to belong to the neighbor's wife, who is also the sister of the woman I am living with. I'm not sure, though—I don't know too much about the family next door. I've only met Harley, the guy I told you about when he helped me with the horse. I don't know what to do with this. Do I keep reading? It kind of feels like an invasion of privacy. If it belonged to Harley's mother, then he should have it, especially considering his mom passed away.*

Casey: Wow, that's full on. If it were me, and because I'm nosey, I'd want to keep reading. When you finish, you could easily apologize and go from there. Is there anything juicy in there?

Mirella: I've only read one entry, and this girl, Olive, has found out she's pregnant by a guy named Ryan and that her parents won't be happy. They would like her to marry the guy next door, William, who I'm guessing is Harley's father. I think I want to keep reading to know Olive and her story.

Casey: So, do that and then hand it over to the neighbor.

Mirella: It feels wrong. I had it with me when I saw Harley earlier, and he didn't say he recognized it or anything. It's been under a bed, covered in dust, in an old cottage that the mother used when she was alive.

Casey: Oh, that's so sad. Maybe read it, and if you feel it contains something they should know, then give it to them and apologize. It's better to ask forgiveness than permission. You and I both know that saying very well.

Mirella: Yes, we do. Anyway, I have to go. I'll message later. The lady here will be mad at me if I don't get back downstairs to help out.

Casey: Okay, but please message me later. I need more of this story.

I don't reply. Instead, I stare down at the notebook. I'll ask Harley some questions tomorrow when I see him, and maybe I'll be able to put more pieces together. Hopefully, he won't mind.

Chapter 7

Mirella

Things didn't go to plan. My heart is broken, and I don't know how I'm going to get through this. I'll be raising a child on my own. Will my family throw me out? This kind of pain is unimaginable. Not even a doctor could stitch me back together. My tears keep falling.

Ryan has gone without a word, which tells me he wants nothing to do with me or the baby. We met at the cottage, and right away, he wanted to get down and play again. He was clearly unhappy about it when I told him I couldn't. When the words, "I'm pregnant," came from my mouth, he laughed—he actually laughed. I've never felt more horrible than I did in that moment. I felt dirty and unclean.

"Is it even mine? How do I know that this isn't some ploy to keep me here? For all I know,

you've been messing around with William. You gave yourself to me so willingly. Maybe you've done it with others." It felt as though I'd been punched in the stomach. He walked out laughing, not listening to me again. I was apparently a liar.

I'd been missing for some time, and no one could find me. I'd collapsed into a heap on the cottage floor and couldn't bring myself to get back up. The wind was knocked out of me. All the ranchers around us were searching. It was William who found me lying on the floor of the cottage on his property. William, though... he knows I like this place.

The conversation we had when he found me is one I'll never forget.

"Has someone harmed you? If they have, I will hurt them." The ferociousness in his tone would surely put fear into anyone. The stone-cold look in his eyes pierced right through me. He cares so much about me.

"No, no one hurt me in the way you're probably thinking. I did this myself and fell into the trap of an unkind man. I'm pregnant, William, and my family is going to hate me for the stupid thing I've done. They'll kick me out, and I'll have nowhere to go."

William's face scrunched up, and he rubbed at his eyes. Then, he glanced up. "Ryan's?" he questioned. I nodded, and that was all he needed. "I guess that explains why he left today before we all realized you were missing. Oh, I wish I could kill him, or at least hurt him in some way."

Ryan left and couldn't care less about me or his baby—although he doesn't believe it is his.

But what William offered next was not what I ever expected.

"What if we got married, and I raised and loved this baby as if it were my own? No judgment. I know your heart belongs somewhere else, but I do hope that, in time, you might come to love me as I have loved you for all these years we have been friends."

I was speechless. I couldn't give him an answer right then. I needed to talk to Dotty. I knew she would help me and give me some solid advice.

William delivered me home to a relieved mother and father. They were ever so grateful to him. I thanked him and told him I'd meet him tomorrow morning at the cottage to talk. With a nod, he left. Watching him leave, I knew he was the man I'd marry. Whether it's love or not, he has offered me something that not even the father of my baby did.

When I told Dotty what had happened and what William had offered, she told me not to take his offer, and I couldn't help but wonder why. I figured it out, though. She's secretly been in love with William and was hoping she would get her chance with him, and now I'm ruining that. I had no idea. She should have said something or made some kind of move for him. Now I'm torn between hurting my sister and letting my family down with my pregnancy. Dotty could always ruin me either way. She knows my secrets. Would she do that, though?

At the end of that tough conversation with her, she said, "Do what you need to." I know *that's not what she wants, but she's aware William has been in love with me for as long as she can remember. He's only ever had eyes for me.*

Why is life so hard? I have a lot to think about and people to consider, especially my sister, but I'll have to make my mind up sooner rather than later if I want to pull this baby off as William's.

More soon,

Olive

"OH, MY GOODNESS," I BREATHE. I'm seeing a movie of this entire book playing out in my head, and I can't help but foresee the outcome. From what I've learned while being here, Dotty and William no longer talk or have anything to do with each other. She doesn't have anything to do with the Rose Ridge family. Her dead sister's children. This is all horrible.

I can't help but wonder if they are aware. Being the bearer of this kind of news would surely make things weird between me and Harley, though. And Harley has never referred to Dotty as his aunt or anything, so I'm assuming he doesn't know they're related.

I'm supposed to go and meet Harley in the next hour or so. I still haven't told Dotty, but I'm going to. After hiding the journal under my pillow, I head out the bedroom door, closing it behind me. Downstairs, Dotty has put some plates out for dinner. My stomach clenches.

Maybe I can head down after I do my jobs. Will Harley wait if I'm a little late?

"Hey, Dotty, do you mind if I go and meet Harley from next door?"

Dotty pauses, her eyes meeting mine. "I don't mind. I can put your plate in the oven for when you get home. Just promise me one thing." She places down the knife she was using to cut up some carrots and turns to face me, her hands placed on her hips. It's something my mother would do when she was going to give me one of *those* talks.

"What's that?"

"You aren't going to end up in a situation I'm going to have to fix. I don't want to do that. As you know very well, I don't have much to do with them next door, so please, don't do anything stupid." She brushes some dark-gray strands of hair from her sun-kissed face.

Olive and the journal entries come rushing to my mind. "I won't do anything stupid. We're just hanging out. I won't be too late. I promise." I swipe my finger over my chest in a cross motion.

"Okay. I've had girls get themselves into trouble before. Not saying it's the kids from next door causing it, but I do know that their daughter Delilah ran off with one of the farmhands, and things didn't work out so well for her then, but I believe things are good now. I don't know too much else."

I cock an eyebrow. Dotty must keep up with what's going on over at the ranch one way or another.

"I won't get myself into trouble. I promise. I'll see you soon. Don't wait up, but I will be back before dark." She nods and goes back to cooking.

I tug a sweater on as it gets cool when the sun disappears. There's probably still a bit of time before Harley arrives, but a walk is what's needed after delving into secrets of the past—Harley's family's past. A part of me wants to tell him and return the journal to him, but I'm worried it will cause trouble in his family. I'm not sure if the family knows about Ryan. I don't think I could do that until I have more information.

I make my way down the now familiar road leading to the cottage and beyond. The birds around me scatter from within the long grass on the side of the road into the air as I walk by. It's so peaceful out here. I can see why country people love it. There's no hustle and bustle of the city, no traffic—nothing to steal these peaceful moments.

My thoughts turn to Olive and how she must have felt dealing with what she had to back then. Being abandoned by the father of her baby. Her sister being in love with the man who was in love with her. That's a Hollywood-worthy storyline right there. I kick a loose rock down the road.

When I glance up, my stomach swirls and dances. Harley is already at the cottage, and he's not alone. He's brought not one but two horses. He hasn't seen me coming as he pats the horses' necks. His mouth moves, but I can't make out what he's saying.

"I'm not getting on that," I call out.

He spins and greets me with a megawatt smile. His black wide-brim hat shades his eyes, and his hair pokes out every which way from underneath it. It's another movie-worthy moment. His stubble is still not shaved, and that's okay. He must live in jeans and tees. I mean, it's all delicious to look at and appreciate. Oh, I fully appreciate the cowboy outfits I've seen on most young men around here. So much better than a suit.

"Come on. Ol' Butter here is the softest horse out there. We have disabled kids riding her. My sister Delilah trained her years ago. Trust me." His last two words ring out like a bell. *Trust him.* Can I trust him not to hurt me?

I slip through the fence and make my way to him, wary of the two large animals standing not far from me. Animals I'm not too keen on.

"I'm not sure I want to ride it. What if it runs off with me on it?"

Harley chuckles. "Butter doesn't run off unless ordered to. Let me teach you how to ride and not be so scared of horses. They are friendly and loving animals, and when we show love to them, they give it back to us in return. Please let me do this for you."

I rub my sweaty hands together and then down my jeans. Suddenly, I don't really need a sweater anymore. The nerves are causing too much heat within me.

Harley drops the reins he was holding, and neither horse moves to run or even walk away. They stay side by side, munching on the grass.

Harley holds out his hand. "Trust me. I won't let anything happen to you." My heart skips a beat, and I take his outstretched hand, squeezing it tightly. "Don't worry. Butter will look after you. I know she will. She's one of our best therapy horses." He moves around them so confidently, with not a worry in the world.

"I'm not sure that even matters to me. My insides are screaming at me right now, telling me to run away."

His thumb glides over the back of my hand, and it momentarily takes away the sheer panic pulsing through every part of my body.

He stops and turns to face me. Releasing my hand, he cups my face with his large, slightly rough hands. I close my eyes briefly and then open them, staring into his dark hazel ones. There's a warmth within them. They look identical to his mother's from the pictures I've seen, though I don't know what color hers were.

I only recognize the shape and the caring nature that pours from them. "I will not let anything happen to you, Mirella. I know this is scary, especially after what happened to you with Dotty's mustang, but I promise you, Butter is nothing like that horse. Come and meet her." Dropping his hands, he reaches for mine, and I let him take one of them.

My heart pounds in my ears with each step I take toward the tall animals. They see us coming toward them, and they start walking our way. I grip Harley's hand tighter and move behind him a little. "Harley, I'm not sure about this," I say breathlessly, fear constricting my throat.

He says nothing but holds out his other hand. The horses stop. He gives them both a good pat on the sides of their faces. They seem to enjoy it.

"Come on, Mirella. This is Butter." Harley pats the lighter-colored chestnut horse. She's smaller than the other one. He pulls my hand around with his, then lets go of my hand and puts it on the bridge of Butter's nose. She doesn't move. She simply stands there, her ears twitching.

I pat her, and she shuffles a little. Harley stands close by, keeping the other horse entertained and happy. "What's your horse's name?" I ask, feeling a little better and slowly warming up to being near Butter.

"This brute is Chester. I trained him. He can still be a handful, but he knows when I'm being serious and to pull himself into line. They are smart animals and only want love and affection. We—and by we, I mean myself and my sister Delilah—have spent years training horses that we've saved from slaughterhouses, or sometimes, people contact us and ask us to take their animals for a price because they are struggling."

"That's so sad. As scared as I am of these two, I'd still hate for anything to happen to them. People can be so cruel sometimes," I mutter, and my parents pop into my head. Maybe they see me as an animal they can just sell off as they please to the person with the most money. I was just a pawn to them, to help their business venture grow. I wasn't their daughter at all.

"That's good to hear. Would you like to try and get on her?" He almost sounds hopeful, and I'm about to burst his bubble.

I shake my head. "No. Not today. Can you tell me more about your sister who helps you with the horses?" Harley is happy to talk about his family.

"Delilah only returned recently. She was with me the day you had your adventure with Dotty's horse." He gives me a sideways glance. It causes my heart to skip a beat.

"Oh, that was your sister?" I remember the blonde woman he was with. The way she appeared so confident on her horse kind of made me jealous. Now I know she trains them, and it all makes sense.

"Yeah, she would probably have that horse of Dotty's in line by now if Dotty would accept some help once in a while." Harley sighs and turns back to Chester. "No one really knows why she won't talk to us or accept our help."

I think I know why, I want to say, but I bite my tongue. Now isn't the time to get into that. He possibly wouldn't believe me, given the fact that I'm new around here.

"She's a hard nut to crack," I say. "Are any of your siblings married?"

Harley releases a loud laugh, and it startles Chester, who nudges Harley with his nose. "Easy, boy, sorry. I didn't mean to scare you. Um, to answer your question, no, none of us are married. Delilah was, and she has a little girl, Olive."

"Olive?" I ask with a start and then realize my mistake. "That's just a different name." I quickly cover the tracks of my outburst.

"Yeah, she's named after our mother."

I was right. The Olive from the journal is his mother, Dotty's sister. I slowly start to put the pieces of this puzzle together.

"Is Delilah the oldest of you and your siblings?" I keep my focus on Butter, and it's funny how a calmness has settled over me with Butter near. But still, if she moved suddenly, I'd probably run away screaming or cower behind Harley and risk looking like a fool.

"No, she's the second oldest. Hudson is the oldest. I mean, he should be married by now — he's thirty-six. I'm surprised he isn't yet, but... oh well, that's his own journey. Nothing to do with me. I'm sure he might think the same as me. Since we've had issues in the past with people in our family choosing the wrong person, we tend to not get involved in each other's love lives. Though, it doesn't stop my sisters from asking questions and probing." He shrugs. "It's what sisters do."

"That's what siblings are for, aren't they?"

"You could say that," he says with a chuckle. "Do you have any siblings?"

I shake my head. "Nope, only child here. I guess that's why my family liked to try and micro-manage everything in my life." Right down to the person I was supposed to marry. I wish they had an older child to focus on instead of just me.

"Is that why you're here? Did they send you to, like, a bootcamp thing? Kidnap you, in a way?"

"Uh, no. That would have actually worked in my favor," I say. I wish things were that easy and not life-changing.

He frowns. "That doesn't sound too good. Hopefully, things get better for you." He reaches out and gives my hand a squeeze. His warmth spreads through me as though I've stepped under a steaming shower.

I turn to him. Our eyes meet. "Things are already getting better. Thanks to you and, of course, Dotty." I smile.

He steps closer and places his hand back on my cheek. His thumb glides over my skin. Each movement ignites a spark within me.

I lean up on my tiptoes. He drops his hand from my face, and I gently press my lips to his cheek. "Thank you for introducing me to Butter and trying to teach me that they aren't bad animals," I whisper against his ear. He doesn't move while I speak, and when I finish, he clears his throat.

He surprises me with a kiss to my own cheek. He smells of wood, pine, and horses. Very cowboy-like. "I wish you would at least sit in the saddle and let me lead you around for a little while." He gestures to Butter.

As scared as I am, I finally say, "Fine, if it will shut you up."

"Yes," he whispers his win.

"Don't get used to it. I won't be on there very long. Now, how do I get up?" I move to the side of Butter and stare at the stirrup. Harley releases Butter's rein.

"Wait, don't you need to hold onto that while I get up so she doesn't move?" I ask, panicked.

"She won't move. Like I said, she's a therapy horse and responds to words and slight nudges to her belly. Watch." He takes my hand, and we move away from Butter. "Butter, come."

Butter's ears turn in our direction, and then she moves toward us, her nose stopping at Harley's chest, giving it a little nudge. He gives her a scratch, and she stays still.

"See? She's really good. Now let's get you up." He guides me back to the side of the horse and taps my left leg. "This foot needs to go in here, and then you're going to hold on here." He touches a horn thing that's on the saddle. "Then, push yourself up with your foot and pull, using that." He taps the horn again.

Seems easy enough. I do what he says and manage to get myself up on the horse. It wasn't this easy last time. Then, I used the fence, and the mustang kept moving around or away from me. Butter doesn't budge with my movements or grunts.

Harley looks up at me like he's proud of me. "There you go. You did it."

"I did, didn't I? Now, how do I get back down?"

He shakes his head, laughing. "You're not getting back down just yet. We're going to go for a little walk around the area here. You agreed." He takes the reins and starts walking. With a click of his tongue, Butter follows.

My body moves with Butter's movements. I stare down at Harley, who has his back to me. His ass is perfect in those jeans.

I mentally slap myself, remembering what Dotty said about getting myself into trouble.

"Are you like this with all girls who come out this way?" I ask.

Harley turns and smiles. "Nope. Usually, I tend to keep business and pleasure separate. My life lately is mostly business. We have a big fundraising fair coming up in a couple of weeks, so the family is preparing for that."

"That sounds really good. What happens there?"

Butter snorts, and we keep walking with Harley leading us. "We raise money to help with things on the ranch. We are self-sufficient, but sometimes it's good to let people know what it is we do out here. We offer a lot of supportive services to those with disabilities or who have been injured in some way, whether it be by accident or if they have served. We have built this place up to be a sanctuary for those who need a place to heal." He speaks so passionately about his ranch and what they stand for.

"It really sounds like a great place to work with and fund." If I had access to money like I once did, I'd put some toward their needs.

"This time around, we have Sebastian King—"

"Wait, you mean the Formula One driver?"

He nods. "Yeah, my sister Delilah is with him."

"Wow, that's so cool." We come full circle, and I say, "Okay, I'm about done please."

Harley stops Butter. "Now, to get off, just lift up with the left foot and bring the other back over and place it on the ground."

I do as he says, but as my foot touches the ground, I lose my balance and stumble back with my left foot still caught in the stirrup.

I drop down and cry out, a sharp pain shooting up my leg that's still in the stirrup. "Oh my… what have I done?"

Chapter 8

Harley

I RACE TO MIRELLA'S SIDE. Butter stays put as I untangle Mirella's foot from the stirrup. She's clearly twisted it the wrong way as she fell, and it was caught—just bent it a little too far.

"This is clearly my own stupid fault." She winces as she moves her left ankle around.

"I'm so sorry. I should have assisted you." Taking her ankle in my hands, I pull off her sneaker.

She hisses slightly. "It's okay. It'll be fine. Just give me a moment. Maybe you could move Butter away a little so I don't risk getting trampled on," she jokes with a weak smile, but I can clearly tell she's not comfortable as she glances up at Butter, fear in her eyes.

Instead of moving the horse, I scoop Mirella up in my arms, and hers go around my neck. I quickly take her to the porch of the cottage. The last bit of daylight kisses the top of the roof as the chilliness of the night begins to set in.

"Really, I am okay. It'll be alright. It's my fault. I don't blame you or Butter," she tries to assure me. I can see she's holding tears back. I've seen this kind of injury more than once in my life, and some can be simple sprain-type things, but others need more attention.

I take a seat beside her and pull her legs up on me to rest and elevate them. "Lean against that post there."

She shuffles and does as I suggest. I touch around her ankle. She is no longer flinching away from me, and I don't know if she's just trying to be brave and put on a front, but I'd rather know if she has seriously injured herself or not. "Please tell me if you're in a lot of pain." I gently rub my hand over her foot, her skin smooth under my touch.

She shrugs and shakes her head. "Honestly, I'm okay. It's got a slight throb to it, but it'll be fine and ready to use again any minute. But I won't be riding again today. I do appreciate you helping me, though. I did have fun, and Butter is a lovely pony. I would gladly give it another go, but only on her."

Placing my hand on her shin, I give it a rub.

"I'd really like that. I can only bring her at the end of the day as she's mostly used for clients, and she rests in between appointments."

"That's okay. So, tell me, why is this place not used anymore? Couldn't it be used as one of your vacation cabins? I know you said it was your mom's, but it seems a shame to leave it to sit and rot away. It's full of dust in there and needs a massive clean." She throws her thumb sideways at the closed door of the cottage. Its chipped paint reminds me of the pain I felt that day as I stepped through it—the day my mother died.

Clearing my throat, I say, "I think we all just feel it holds too much personal history, and it's a small piece of Mom that we hold close. She loved it out here almost as much as she loved the library in the homestead."

Mirella perks up. "You have a library?"

"We do. My sister Delilah has asked me to not let our father close it up. When she left a couple of years ago, it wasn't pretty, and Dad covered everything up and then shut the door. No one was allowed in there again."

"Um, wow. That's crazy. What's your dad's name?" she asks out of the blue. That's not usually something someone asks, but I guess she's new around here and doesn't know everyone personally. I'm sure my sisters would love to meet her.

"His name is William. Big ol' broody William. Some call him a grump and others a teddy bear — depends on who you talk to. I'm sure Dotty refers to him as something else — something more colorful," I state.

"I have no idea. In fact, I can't remember her mentioning his name at all the entire month or so I've been here." She rubs her bandage free hand down her legs and gives her injured foot a little movement. She doesn't wince in pain this time, thankfully.

Glancing up at the now pink-orange sky, I'm reminded of *that* day. It was this exact time of day my father had sent me up here to collect Mom. She'd wanted some peace away from the hustle and bustle of the ranch, and so, because she was sick, I'd driven her up here. We'd had this place stocked with her favorite snacks and drinks. Oh, that reminds me.

Gently, I place Mirella's legs down, step from the porch step, and go to the side of the cottage to the power box. I open it and flick the switch, and every light that had been left on comes to life.

I sit back down and lift her legs back over mine.

"Wow, I didn't realize there was power out here. I thought it was one of those old places that might crumble at any moment," Mirella says as her eyes roam over the cottage once again.

"No, it's been maintained by one of my sisters, and Hudson comes out to make sure the wiring is all clean and no vermin have gotten into it every now and then. Maybe one day, when the time is right, it'll get used again."

"Could it be our meeting place?" Mirella asks, catching me off-guard.

Silence takes hold of me, and I'm caught in a trance, staring at that door again—one I've not opened since the day I left, carrying my mother in my arms, practically lifeless.

Warmth touches my hand. I jerk it away, and Mirella jerks hers away, too. "I'm so sorry," I say hurriedly, reaching for her hand.

"I'm sorry. We don't have to meet here again if you don't want to." Her cheeks pink, and she moves her legs from mine but keeps hold of my hand. My chest tightens, the emotions from the past strangling me.

"It's not anything you've said or done." I move closer to her. Her warmth and presence take away the sting of the memory that threatens to tip me over the edge. "I'm sorry," I say, rubbing her hand, amazed at how easy it is to get close to her, for her to allow me into her personal space. "Mirella, I feel strangely close to you. I don't know why, but something's different when I'm with you."

She squeezes my hand. "I get it. It's new to me as well, but we don't have to rush into anything. You didn't give up, even when Dotty told you to because she was protecting me."

My brows knit together. "What is she supposed to be protecting you from? Surely, I wasn't that scary that day?" I give a small wink, and she blushes and turns her eyes away, looking out into the darkness that's overcome our properties.

She waves her hand. "No, I think it's just Dotty. Do you know if she has family or not? I don't see a lot of people around her place unless they are looking to buy something or helping with something, and none of them are her family." Our fingers entangle together, and she glides her thumb over my rough callouses, not fazed at all.

Her question about Dotty interests me. "Now that you mention it, I don't recall her having family. I remember someone, perhaps it was one of the neighbors, who said she had a sister, but they never told me who, and I've never seen or heard of any family coming to visit."

Mirella nods at this information as though something is on her mind.

"Why do you ask?"

"No reason. Was just wondering about the woman I live with. She's a vault."

"I understand that. My father is the same. Wait until you meet him."

Her head jerks up and in my direction. "Meet him?" She almost sounds panicked.

"Yeah, if you come to a bonfire or the fundraiser, then he'll be there, and so will the rest of my siblings. I'd love for you to meet them."

She nods. "Okay. That sounds good." She doesn't sound too sure, though.

"Don't worry. They won't bite either. Most likely, they'll grill you with twenty questions," I tease, and she shoves me in the shoulder with her own.

"That I can handle." A silence falls between us, and all I can hear is the horses munching away on the grass and snorting occasionally. The crickets and other night creatures come alive. "It really is peaceful out here. I wish I could stay here forever."

Her words startle me. "Are you not planning to stay?"

"I don't know what my long-term plan is. Being at Dotty's is only meant to be short-term until I figure out another option and things with my family settle down—not that I plan to ever be under their roof again in the foreseeable future."

"Oh, okay. Maybe I can persuade you to stay a little longer." I wiggle my eyebrows playfully and give her hand another squeeze.

With Mirella, I feel as though a curveball has been thrown at me. I never expected her to be someone I could possibly open up to. Sometimes, there are people who make it so easy to let everything out, to talk about Mom with. Not even my family knows how that day has affected me. I've just dealt with it the best I could. It's been years, and I should be past it by now, but I don't know how to let go of those emotions.

"Maybe," is all Mirella says, and that simple word is enough to stir up some hope within me.

Another hour passes. We talk freely and enjoy one another's company.

"I better get back. I told Dotty I wouldn't be late, and after my day, I'm pretty tired," Mirella says and gets up, testing her foot, which seems to be okay. She goes and collects her shoe, which is something I should have done. How stupid of me.

"Sorry. I could have gotten that for you." I rush to her side.

"No, it's okay. I needed to test the ankle anyway. It feels good. Slightly sore, but I don't think it's anything serious, which is a good sign. Next time, I'll know what not to do, and that's lose my footing while climbing down."

"I mean, we could always try bareback another time, and you'll have nothing to get tangled on," I offer. "I can't say it's comfortable, but it's still nice."

"We'll see. I'm in no rush to get back on." She takes a seat on the porch and puts her sneaker back on. I don't want this night to be over, but I think it's for the best.

"Here. I have something for you." I head over to Chester's saddle bag and grab out the piece of folded paper that has my number on it. I hand it to her, and she willingly takes it. "It's my number, so now if you don't contact me, I'll know where I stand."

Giving her a wink, I lean over to peck her on the cheek, but she's preoccupied with the note and turns to say something as I get close, so instead of me kissing her cheek, our mouths connect, and there are fireworks. Electrifying and completely unexpected.

Her soft, lush lips press against mine.

I quickly pull away. "I'm so sorry. I wasn't going in for your lips."

Mirella smiles and raises her hand, pressing it to my mouth to stop me from talking. "It's okay," she says softly.

"I don't regret it, though," I blurt out.

Her laughter fills the night, and it makes my chest swell with affection for her. She is beautiful. Her dark hair falls out of her messy bun that sits high on her head, and her pink lips are tempting and inviting all at the same time. I want to kiss her again.

Chapter 9

Mirella

THAT WAS UNEXPECTED, BUT WOW, mind-blowing.

"I don't regret it either," I say softly. I'd do it again for the burst of sensations it gave me. Is this what it's supposed to feel like with someone a person would care about? I mean, I've kissed boys before — plenty — but none of them ever felt like this. When I kissed the man my parents wanted me to marry, that was like kissing a brick wall. No emotions. No fireworks. Nothing.

This, with Harley, was something else. It was magical, even though it was cut short when he pulled away in shock. I would have done the same if it were me. I'm glad it was him, though. It shows me the kind of person he is.

"Anyway, I guess I better go. Thank you for the

short riding lesson." Rising from the porch, I tuck Harley's note into my jeans and tap my legs.

Harley stands there in front of me. The look on his face tells me he's warring with himself over something—that and the way he glances at me and then at the ground.

Taking a step closer, I take his scruffy face in my hands and pull him in for a proper kiss, and it is even more powerful than the last one, weakening my legs. His arms wrap around my waist, securing me safely against his solid body.

His tongue invades my mouth, and I let it. After a moment, the kiss slows, and finally, he gives me one last brush across my lips, lifting his head slightly. The sparkle in his eyes could light my way home—it's that bright. My eyes probably mirror his.

"I wasn't expecting that, but I wanted it," he says, resting his forehead against mine.

"Where's your hat?"

"The ground. I didn't want it to get in the way of that epic kiss. Can I walk you home, and then I'll come back for the horses?" He tightens his grip around me. It's a surreal feeling when someone holds you and doesn't seem to want to let you go.

"Sure, if the horses are going to be okay?"

"They'll be fine." He releases me and picks up his hat. He places it back on his head even though the sun has well and truly disappeared.

We silently slip through the fence and make our way back down toward Dotty's. Harley reaches out, taking my hand in his. No words need to be spoken.

"Hey, did your mom have any family that you guys all hang out with or who helps on the ranch?"

Harley shakes his head. "Mom never spoke of anyone. Though, now that I think about it, we would ask, but she'd change the subject. That's weird, right?"

"Sounds a little weird," I respond.

"We were kids, and I guess as we grew up we were caught up in our own family. There are a lot of us kids, and we took up a lot of Mom's time, and the ranch took up a lot of Dad's time. We just assumed she was an only child because she never mentioned anyone. When Odette came along and my parents realized she needed some extra help and attention, that was what we all focused on. Odette is much better now, and we all know how to help her."

"Oh, what was wrong with Odette?"

"She's disabled, but it doesn't stop her from loving life. She's one special girl and completely blunt with you as she has no filter. That's what I love most about her — her honesty."

"I can only imagine what it's like. I'm sure she's a special girl, though." I never want to say the wrong thing when it comes to people with disabilities. I want to help all of them. I want to help those who can't get the help they need. I never know how or where to start, though. Perhaps this is a chance for me to rediscover what I'm meant to do with my life other than party it away on rooftops and get drunk with my friends.

Being out here with Dotty and now Harley has really taught me so much already about the real world and the challenges people face on a daily basis. Not everyone gets everything handed to them. That's been my life, and I don't want it anymore.

"Odette really is special. She has a boyfriend, Devon, who works at the ranch as well." Harley sounds so proud.

I turn to him. "That's amazing," I say.

Harley chuckles. "Yeah, he's a great guy. His sister comes out here often to check on him, and it's great to see him with her."

"That's cool." The house comes into view, and Dotty has left the back light on and the one in the kitchen. Everything else seems to be shut off. "Well, this is me. It looks like Dotty has gone to bed."

We stop on the rise before the homestead and turn to face each other. "Did she know you were coming to see me tonight?" Harley asks.

I nod. "Yep. She just made me promise to not get myself into trouble. A part of me thinks she was talking from past experience."

He shrugs. "I have no idea. Your guess would probably be more accurate than mine."

"I think we're both in the dark there. Anyway, thanks for tonight. I had fun even though I looked like a fool falling over." I shuffle closer to him, and he grins, then places his hands on my hips.

"I'm just glad you're okay and not seriously hurt." He reaches up with one hand and removes his hat before leaning in for one last kiss of the night. He even tastes like the pines. That's weird, but also, it's him. It's so Harley.

He steps back and replaces his hat. I can't see his face very well thanks to the cover of his hat and the darkness of the night. The sky is clear, with stars lighting it up, only there's no moon, so it's darker than usual. "Message me or I'm going to come and bother Dotty again. Which would you prefer?" he asks.

"I think I'd like to see you try and get past Dotty again," I tease.

"Yeah, of course you would. Playing hard to get. Okay, then. I won't give up, though."

"That's what I'm hoping." With one last kiss, I take off toward the house. When I turn around, Harley still stands there. He throws up his hand and waves. The grin that spreads across my face is one I'm unsure will ever come off. Harley has changed something within me, and I like it. I like him and the side of me he brings out. The way he managed to get me on that horse and then took care of me when I'd stupidly hurt myself was amazing. I want more nights and moments like we shared. I've never felt more seen or heard in my entire life.

I feel so sick. I don't know if it's just my nerves or the pregnancy—but surely it wouldn't be that so soon. It's been one day since William offered to help me, and I'm so scared to say yes. If I say yes, then I risk Dotty hating me, but if I don't agree, then I'm left dealing with the anger my parents are going to throw in my direction, and who knows what else? They could kick me out. I'd like to think that wouldn't happen, but my father is a man whose attitude can flip so easily.

I could just run away, but to where? I have no money or any way of actually getting out of here. The nearest big town is two hours away. I really have no other choice than to accept William's offer. I hate that I've put him in this position, and I hate what this is going to cause between Dotty and me.

William and I are supposed to meet later to figure things out. Won't it seem suspicious to our families that, all of a sudden, we're engaged, and we want to get married right away? Couldn't we just elope? That would be the best option. Then, we could say that we've been married longer than we originally state to everyone else.

Well, instead of hashing this out in my journal, I better go and talk to Dotty. I hope she understands.

More soon,

Olive

I could seriously write a book based on Olive's life and the trials she is facing. I'm not pregnant out of wedlock, and even if I were, it's a different time compared to what it was back then for her. With the parent thing, I completely understand.

I reach for my phone and send Casey a message.

Mirella: *Hey Cas, well, guess what??*

Casey: *WHAT?*

Mirella: *I kissed the guy next door, and he got me back on a horse.*

Casey: *Um, who are you, and what have you done with the other Mirella?*

Mirella: *Ha ha. He gave me his number, and I still haven't contacted him, even though it's been a couple of days. I don't want to come across as desperate.*

Casey: *You better message him soon. Why are you worried about coming across as desperate? I'm sure he gave you his number so YOU CAN CONTACT HIM, silly! Message him right now.*

Mirella: *I'm not sure. What if he's changed his mind? It's not like he's been knocking on my door.*

Casey: *Shut up and message him.*

I know she's right, but I'm usually the one getting chased, not the other way around. My world has really gone topsy-turvy.

My heart races as I grab the note from the bedside table where I'd put it the other night when I got back.

Mirella: Hey, it's Mirella. Sorry for the delay in messaging. I didn't want to come across as too desperate or something.

I release the breath I was holding and message Casey back.

Mirella: It's done. I'm not sure what kind of person he is with a phone and if he keeps it on him or not, or if he messages regularly.

Casey: Either way, at least you gave it your best shot. And besides, he might take a while to reply because of work. I look forward to the day when I hopefully get to meet this Harley guy. Look at what he's got you doing. He's a miracle worker, if I do say so myself.

Mirella: I'm not sure he'd be working right now since it's nighttime. Usually, once the sun goes down, most of the work stops unless it's an emergency of some sort. The things you learn.

Casey: In that case, he should get back to you sooner rather than later. I'm gonna go because this past weekend has worn me out. Time for some sleep.

Mirella: Okay. I'll talk to you later.

After throwing my phone on my bed, I head downstairs. The television is going in the living room, but I head to the kitchen and grab an apple from the fruit bowl, needing a top-up after dinner. When I glance up, I let out a little squeal and drop my apple.

I stare through the window of the back door, illuminated by the porch light, and see Harley standing there.

"What's wrong?" Dotty calls as her footsteps come from the living room in the direction of the kitchen.

"What are you doing?" I whisper to Harley who stays by the closed back door.

"What are you screaming at, Mirella?" Dotty comes around the corner and spots Harley. Turning to me, she wears a slight scowl on her face. "What's *he* doing here?"

"I don't know. He was just here when I looked up," I answer hurriedly, nerves tightening my stomach.

"Well, figure it out," she huffs and turns back toward the living area, the scowl still on her face.

I race to the door. Opening it, I say, "Why are you here?"

"I told you that if I didn't hear from you, I'd come visit." He shrugs and shoves his hands in his jeans pockets.

"I messaged you," I say.

"What, like, five minutes ago? It was too late by then. I was already on my way here. I did say that I would go to Dotty again." He shrugs but still gives me one of those grins.

I take a bite from my apple and simply stare at him, then finally say, "You still haven't told me why you're here? You could have easily come during the day and not scared the heck out of me."

"Come with me. I'm taking you somewhere. Grab your sweater and your sneakers. Let's go." He waves me along in a *hurry-up* gesture.

"What? Right now?"

"Yes. Go get yourself ready, and I'll wait here." Taking my shoulders, he turns me around and gives me a gentle push back in the direction of the kitchen.

My feet manage to start moving on their own again, and I'm left walking up the stairs, stunned. Why would he be here?

The exhilaration of the unknown lights a spark within me. Where are we going?

Chapter 10

Harley

I WATCH AS SHE TURNS away. I close the door so as not to let cool air inside, and I wait on the porch. I've never been on Dotty's porch. In fact, I've never even had the chance to knock on her door. She's always outside during the day. I glance to the right. Something catches my eye, coming up beside me.

"What are your intentions with Mirella?" Dotty stands beside me, her arms crossed over her chest. Not sure if it's meant to be standoffish or if she's just trying to keep warm. I didn't even hear the door.

I clear my throat. Suddenly, I'm nervous because I'm actually having a civil conversation with Dotty, the grumpy neighbor, as we've grown up to know her. "Um, I like hanging out with her. She's a great girl."

"A great girl..." she repeats more slowly. "That doesn't really answer my question. Are you expecting more from her? She's here for a reason, and that's for me to look out for her until she can move on."

My brows knit together at her words. "Move on? Like, she is planning to leave at some point?" It's as though someone has taken a pin to the happy balloon I'd had floating around a moment ago. Even though Mirella has told me this information, it seems more real coming from Dotty. Part of me hopes she'll stay a while longer. "Why are you looking out for her and not her family? Dotty, what's going on?" I ask. Worry rips through me like a desert storm, the sand tearing up all thoughts I'd previously had about her possibly staying. What is her story?

Dotty rubs her forehead and sighs. "It's not my place to say anything, but I don't want you getting her hopes up only to shoot them down. All men are the same. Mirella is welcome to stay as long as she wants."

It's as though she's talking in riddles. Some of this makes sense, but the rest is like gibberish. "Dotty, I will always look out for and protect Mirella. I'm not here to cause her any harm. It's not my intention. If you'd give me and my family a chance, you'd probably actually see that we aren't the enemy and have only ever tried to be polite to you."

She scoffs. "Maybe your parents never told you the truth."

"What?" I start and am cut off by the door behind us closing and Mirella coming to my side.

"What, what?" Mirella glances between Dotty and me.

"Nothing, dear. I'll leave a light on for you." Dotty's icy eyes connect with mine, and she says, "Don't have her out too late please. She has a big day tomorrow."

I give a stiff nod, still seething over Dotty's last words. What did she mean? *Maybe my parents never told me the truth.* What truth is she talking about?

Dotty disappears back inside, and Mirella and I are left standing on the back porch.

"What's wrong? What did she say to you?" Mirella's gentle touch on my arm startles me back to the present. I stop stewing over Dotty and her words.

"Oh, don't worry about it. She's just making sure I'm not taking advantage of you." I wink. "Come on. I've got a surprise for you." Reaching out, I take her hand in mine and lead her back up the dirt road heading toward the cottage.

"Where are you taking me?"

"You'll see." We finally slip through the fence, and I lead her to my waiting truck. I open the passenger door for her, and she slips in. It's the perfect night for this—there's still a little bit of light, but it's not super bright.

I jump in and turn the engine over.

"Can I just say that I'm glad it's not a horse this time?" she says with a small laugh.

"Don't worry. That's not over yet. I'll get you back on another horse. You'll be a pro by the time I'm finished with you." I'd spend my days with her if I wasn't so busy helping Dad and training the horses. "Hey, I wanted to ask you. If you aren't busy this weekend, I'd like you to come to the bonfire. You remember the one I told you about that we do with the guests and workers?"

She nods. It's then I really notice and take in her appearance. Her hair is loose around her shoulders, the darkness really bringing out her eyes and making her lips stand out equally as much. She has beauty like I've never seen before.

"That should be okay," she replies.

"Great. I'll pick you up on Friday night. Will Dotty mind?"

"Well, she wasn't too keen to see you tonight, was she? But she'll get over it." Mirella glances out the window as I head to the back part of our property lines.

The ride is silent as I drive along the familiar dirt road. Finally, we come over a small ridge, and I am greeted with a beautiful sight.

"Wow." I hear Mirella breathe.

Before us is a big pond with a small waterfall with fresh water coming off the hill beside it. Small trees surround the pond with a good amount of space between each tree.

"Welcome to one of my many favorite spots. This one, though, is my ultimate nighttime one." I pull in and put the car in park, and we sit in silence once again. I haven't been out here in a while, especially since it's mostly cool at night now.

"Is this where you bring all the ladies?" she teases and slaps my arm. I catch her hand in mine.

"This is where I bring only the special ladies, and let me tell you, there haven't been many of them. Working on a ranch and away from civilization isn't where I meet a whole lot of women. That's why you're so special. There's only one of you, and from the moment I saw you, I was sold."

Mirella's head drops, but I don't miss the smile that shifts the corner of her mouth. "I can't say I've ever really been special to anyone, even my own family." Her voice catches, and the protective male within me wants to hurt those who have hurt her.

"Do you think you'll ever feel comfortable enough to talk to me about what brought you all the way to Dotty's and not living the high life in New York City? Wouldn't you rather be doing whatever it is people do there? Isn't it the party place?" That's my way of trying to find out more about her in a subtle-yet-not-so-subtle way.

Mirella says nothing but pushes her door open and climbs out. I follow and keep step beside her as she walks down to the pond's edge where she stops and stares out into the rippling water. The sound of the waterfall hitting the pond has always been soothing for me, especially after I lost Mom.

She speaks quietly. "I do miss New York. It's been my home for my entire life. I haven't known anything different, so to be here..." She gestures around us. "I'm learning a lot about the rest of the world and also about myself. I was the party girl, and here, I'm the helping hand, and that's fine with me. The whole 'what brought me here' bit is another story. I don't want to talk about that right now. I don't want to ruin this moment." She hugs herself and sits down on the grass.

I sit down, putting my legs on either side of her and wrapping her in my arms from behind. I bury my head in her hair that smells of strawberry and citrus. "You could never ruin this moment. I hope I'm not coming on too heavy for you. If I am, just tell me to back off, and I will. I don't want to make you feel uncomfortable in any way."

Leaning back, she rests her head on my chest and says, "I'm content. I've never felt more at ease with anyone in my life. I've been taught to be and act a certain way, and the simplicity and joy I feel while hanging out with you is new yet exciting for me. If I felt uncomfortable, you'd know because I'd be back at Dotty's and not here with you." She sounds dreamy.

"That's good to know."

We're silent a moment before she says, "Are there many people going to the bonfire this Friday?"

"The usual—maybe thirty people including my family, the other ranch workers, and some guests. Not all the guests come. Some just like to keep to themselves, and that's totally okay," I offer and tighten my arms around her a little more, wanting to freeze this moment in time.

"So, a good number of people. What's one more, then, right?"

"Exactly. Dotty mentioned to me earlier that you were possibly only here for a short time, and I know you mentioned that the other day, but are you really planning to go?" My heart pounds in my chest, and I'm sure she can feel the vibration on her back.

She inhales a deep breath and releases it. "I don't know what's going to happen. For now, just know that I like it here, and I'm not planning on going anywhere until Dotty wants to throw me out. If you keep showing up unannounced, then she might do just that." She chuckles, and I tickle her, causing her to jump and twist slightly so that she is now half-facing me. Our eyes lock, and my heart races. I can't wait to kiss her and taste her.

Chapter 11

Mirella

THE INTENSITY IN HIS GAZE is blazing. He wants to kiss me again, and I don't plan on saying no.

"Mirella, just know that I'm not ever going to hurt you," he says.

"That's something that will have to be proven," I say as I recall Olive's journal and what she experienced with Ryan. Harley is clearly not Ryan, but when this thing between us begins to grow more and people get involved, it could become ugly. People can be judgy, and whether they're out to be hurtful or not, someone could get hurt.

"I will prove it," he whispers and leans in, one of his hands cupping my cheek, my body coming to attention with his caress. I ache for his mouth on mine, and I close the small distance between us. Our mouths crash together. Harley pulls me around and lays me down as he hovers over the top of me. Our hands roam each other's bodies. We make small touches that ignite so much passion between two strangers. It's only a matter of time before this becomes a wildfire, and one of us could end up burnt.

I gently push him back, our chests moving in tandem with each heavy breath we take. Want scorches his eyes. His hand rests under my shirt on the bare skin of my belly. My body begs for his touch.

"I'm sorry if I took it too far," he says hurriedly. "Ugh, I seem to be doing this all wrong with you. I don't want it to only be physical between us. My mother taught me better than that." He huffs and lies down beside me, his hands resting on his stomach, my body cold with the loss of his touch.

I'm the one keeping secrets from him and pushing him away. If anything, it's going to be me who hurts him. When the day comes that I hand over that journal, I don't know if I'm going to turn his or his brother's life upside down, given that Hudson is the older brother. Guilt washes over me as though I've been doused in ice-cold water.

I move to the same position as him and stare up at the stars, their twinkling a reminder that no matter how ugly the world can be, there's always beauty in the darkness if you're looking hard enough.

Harley rolls on his side. "All right, how about we get to know each other a little better? I won't ask you about certain things, as I can tell you're still not sure about trusting me, and that's okay. You can go first." He reaches out and takes my hand.

I wrack my brain and try to think of a not-too-invasive question. "Okay, I have one. Will you ever leave the ranch?"

"Oh, that's a tough one." He falls on his back, his breath rushing from him. After a moment, he says, "I'd like to say yes, but I really feel the answer might be no, I won't leave."

"Why's that?" I thought for sure he'd leave, but maybe things are different out here.

"The ranch is my family's legacy. I want my kids—when I eventually have them—to learn that people in the world, though they may come across as different sometimes, are all special and need love and support. Plus, I think kids need to learn what hard work is." He comes across as knowing exactly what he wants for his future children, and I can't say it's bad.

"That's cool." Lying there, I twist my head in his direction to find him watching me. "Your turn," I say with a small smile.

"My turn. What shall I ask? Okay, here's one. What's your favorite ice cream?"

I burst out laughing. "Ice cream? That's your question?"

"Yeah, I need to know the small things about you as well. That way, I can find new ways to spoil and spend time with you." He winks and runs his fingers through his hair to get it out of his face. He's not wearing his cowboy hat, but he's just as hot.

"All right, my favorite ice cream is chocolate-chip cookie dough."

"Nice, Mabel likes that one."

"Mabel is one of your sisters?"

"Yeah, she is. One of the nosey ones, but I'd have to say I'm closer with Delilah and Hudson. Still, the others are great as well, and I'd do anything for them."

"That's sweet."

We continue to play the game, and by the end of it, I know his favorite color, food, ice cream flavor, how he hates when Hudson chews with his mouth open sometimes, and how Delilah is going to be here soon, and the list goes on. Mix all those questions with flirtatious touches and the odd kiss here and there, and it's weird for me to admit—and I'd only admit it to myself at the moment—but I'm smitten with Harley.

He offers me something no other guy in my life ever has. He makes me feel heard. Like I matter. And most of all, he doesn't force me to answer anything or demand I do something or agree with him.

"I better get you home, or Dotty is going to kill me."

I grin. "Maybe not kill you—that's a bit dramatic. She really is a nice lady. You just have to give her a chance."

Harley gets up off the grass and holds out his hands. "I would if she gave me a chance."

I take his hands, and he pulls me up and wraps his arms around me. We stand there for a moment, enjoying the embrace.

"Come on." He leads me back to the truck, and we head back to the cottage.

Dotty hates me. She told me she'll never talk to me again. How much more damage can I cause? My parents haven't picked up on the tension between Dotty and me yet, but it's only a matter of time.

In other news, I met and spoke with William. I accepted his offer. Now we have to put plans into motion to tell our parents and make them believe that we are smitten with each other. Heck, we even had to practice some kind of kiss. I feel nothing for him. I do hope that changes over time. I could come to love him and grow old with him, but will Dotty forgive me?

William, I think, really does care about me, and I'd hate to hurt his feelings if, at the end of all of this, we didn't make it. I will do my best to grow my feelings that were there between us in the beginning, before Ryan came along, and care for him. He deserves it.

Before we left the cottage, he said, "Olive, I will spend my days trying to get you to fall in love with me. I do care about you and this baby, even though it isn't mine. I'm here for you, and we're in this together. Always together." He leaned over and gave me a small kiss on my cheek. That was the moment a tiny spark kicked into life, as though a new star had decided to show up in the sky, a representation of something new with the possibility of it being big and bright.

I'm so thankful to him for what he is putting on the line for my child. I'll never be able to repay him.

Now, to tell our parents.

More soon,

Olive

It almost sounds like she was forced to be with him. Thankfully, William was a good man and took good care of her, and they ended up having a happy life by the looks of it. They had more kids together, and that wouldn't have happened if they didn't grow to love each other in the end.

Hudson is the oldest, so he must be this Ryan's son. I wonder if Ryan ever came back or wanted anything to do with him. Shame on him. He doesn't deserve to know him—not after what he did to Olive and Hudson.

My phone vibrates, alerting me to a message. As I pick it up, Harley's name pops up.

Harley: *Thanks for the night last night. It was fun. I hope you have a good day doing whatever it is Dotty has you doing.*

Mirella: *It was fun last night. Thanks for surprising me and dragging me out. Things around here were pretty boring and lonely until you showed up.*

Harley: *Technically, you showed up on my property in the early hours of the morning, and the rest is now history.*

Mirella: *Again, sorry about that.*

Harley: *Ha ha, don't worry. You wouldn't be saying sorry if you didn't get caught, but I'm glad you did, or we wouldn't be talking right now, and that would be a dang shame.*

He is right. If I didn't do what I did, then I wouldn't be experiencing these feelings for him. It's like he's caught me in his trap, and I don't want to escape. And as I learn more about his mom and her story, it draws me closer to her and Harley, even though he's not in the actual journal.

Her last entry was just over ten years ago, and from what Harley has told me, it's close to the time when she passed away.

Mirella: *It would be a shame. Thanks for not getting angry at me like you could have, considering I wasn't very nice to you when we first met.*

Harley: *I'll let that slide. I'd say you were under some stress, given your ordeal, which I won't mention again. I'm just glad we've got a second chance now of sorts. Do you think you would have sought me out if I didn't catch you on our property?*

Mirella: I don't know. I don't really know how I would have seen you. I mean, I could have saved you from Dotty's wrath when you came by to check on me, but everything was and still is so new to me. With everything I've been going through with my family, I didn't need any extra stress, but hey, I got that stress now. LOL!

Harley: I'm not stressful! What are your plans today?

Mirella: Doing the horse stalls again, cleaning them out. Raking and cleaning out the chicken coop. All those fun things. What about you?

Harley: I've got to go put in some time with the new horse we got. She's a beauty but needs some TLC. I saved her from the slaughterhouse. Then, I have to help out with some therapy and clean down the horses—all the fun things around here.

Mirella: Do you have to have a degree to work with the people you do and to conduct their therapy?

Harley: Yeah, I did my courses from home so I could still help out around here, and when I passed, Dad gave me permission to do therapies and other things. I enjoy it.

It's possible this could be something I could do. I could learn to stand on my own two feet a bit more. It would be good having this kind of thing under my belt. College was always the party phase of my life, but now I need something more—something that helps those who need it.

Mirella: That's cool. Maybe it's something I should look into since I don't really have anything else going for me, and I think this kind of work is something I'd really enjoy.

Harley: I can help you get set up on the courses if you want and even show you around here to help do the odd job and earn some extra cash. I'm not sure if Dotty is paying you or what kind of arrangement you have, but I'd be happy to help and talk to my dad about something. Even cleaning the cottages people vacation in when they leave would be a great assistance, kind of like housekeeping. At the moment, Sybil, one of my sisters, is doing it on her own, and I think she could use some help. What do you think?

Talk about an overload of offers and information. Am I going to be around long enough for these offers to work for me? I'd hate to start and leave Harley in the lurch.

Mirella: Thanks for all the suggestions and help. I think I would like a hand with the courses. My only problem is that I probably don't have the money for it right now.

I think about the small amount of cash I took from my bank account the day before I left. It hasn't dwindled, but it hasn't grown either.

Harley: I don't mean to pry, but does Dotty pay you?

Mirella: No, I work to pay for my rent and food. I have a little cash but not enough to cover the cost of schooling.

Harley: *Okay, we can figure something out. Don't worry. I better go and get back to work. Lots to do and not enough daylight. I'll talk to you later.*

Mirella: *Sounds good. Have a good one.*

It's nice finally being able to talk to new people, and I'm eager to meet more at the bonfire this coming Friday. Hopefully, one of his sisters is nice enough. Meeting his father is another thing I'm looking forward to. I have been wondering what he is like now compared to what I've been reading about in Olive's journal.

Chapter 12

Harley

"I'M SURPRISED YOU'RE HERE AND not running off with your mystery girl," Tally jeers as I step into the kitchen. It's a late start for me today, and Dad might be annoyed at that, but for Tally to have a go at me is something else.

I snatch up one of the scones she's baked and smother it with jelly and cream. "What's your problem?" I snap back before I take a bite.

Tally is an amazing baker. Our home is forever smelling of freshly baked cakes and cookies. It's a miracle we all haven't needed to go on diets given the amount of sugar she loves to put into her sweets. I wouldn't want it to change, though. I love everything she makes.

She sprinkles more flour on the countertop,

and then her cold stare meets my gaze, her ice-blue eyes as cold as she is in this moment. "None of your business."

"It is my business when you're having a go at me for something I know nothing about. So, I'll ask again. What's wrong?"

Tally continues with finishing off the last of her scone dough and cutting out the round shapes, placing them on a waiting cooking tray. "It's just one of those days. Dad is in a mood, Hudson pretends he doesn't notice Dad's mood, Odette seems to be more agitated over things that normally don't bother her, Sybil — well, she's Sybil and Little Miss Perfect. Then, there's Mabel, who seems to have it all together, and here I am, slaving away in the kitchen once again while everyone else has their fun, and you get to run off with the girl from next door. I just feel like the odd one out here."

There it is. Tally has always somehow managed to be the angriest of all of us — apart from Dad. She struggles to connect with others sometimes, and she takes it all out on us, her family.

I place the last bit of scone in my mouth, take the few steps over to her, and pull her away from the counter and into a hug. "You're doing amazing, Tally, and I'll let you in on a little secret."

"What's that?" she grumbles into my shoulder, given I'm taller than her.

Lowering my voice to a whisper, I say, "Delilah and Olive are coming home in a few days."

She pulls back, her frown changing into a wide grin. "What? When?"

"She hasn't given me a solid date, but knowing her style, she'll just show up." I release Tally and take a step back.

Tally adores Olive, our niece. When Delilah came back home, Tally and she didn't see eye-to-eye on a lot of things until Delilah revealed what the past three years had been like for her and Olive. Thankfully, Delilah and Tally get along better now. Not great, but better.

"I should get busy making all of Olive's favorite things. I know they've only been gone a short while, but I miss Olive. Having a little person around the house changes things so much, and I really like it." She gets back to what she was doing by brushing some milk over the scones, and with a simple confession about Delilah and Olive, Tally's mood has changed, which is good to see.

Tally has been battling her own demons, figuring out where she belongs in the grand scheme of things around the ranch. A small part of me feels like she wants to maybe go away for a little while to learn to grow on her own. I can only imagine what Dad would have to say about that. He doesn't like it when we talk about leaving.

Since Mom died, it's been him raising us, and when Delilah left, it broke him. He wasn't the same person for a long time, and even to this day, he isn't. He must have some big demons he keeps bottled up. When they get cracked open, an avalanche of emotions slides on through the house, and we all have to try and ski through it without collecting each other and hurting one another.

"I get what you mean, Tally. Olive has changed the dynamic of things around here. Wait for the day when we've all got someone, and we all start having kids of our own. Those are going to be some amazing times."

"Pfft, I have to actually meet someone first, and I don't know if you have looked around here lately, but there are slim pickings in the future-husband department. I have plans, but I'm just not sure when I want to execute them." She shrugs and slides a new tray into the oven.

Her words cause me to pause as I layer up another scone. "What plans? I'm all for plans and helping."

"I can only imagine what Dad would think."

"I learned my lesson with Dee. I won't let people get held back, even if it means they have to leave for a short period of time to be able to discover themselves. It's clear that it worked for Delilah, even though she had to go through hell and back. If I would have known..." My words trail off, and anger floods through me at the mere thought of Eli, Delilah's deceased ex-husband.

Tally's hand covers mine. "I'm sure we all would have been there if we'd known, no matter what had transpired in the past between us. I think we have our own lessons to learn, and that was one of hers. Now, she's got Sebastian and his girls. They have their hands full. Even though it's all new to both of them, I see more kids in their future. Don't dwell on Eli and what happened. Nothing good can come of it," Tally says softly.

Her words hit me. She is right. We all have our own lessons to learn. That's life. Life isn't meant to be all sunshine and rainbows. We all know that the brightest rainbows come out after big storms.

"You're right. I'm here if you need help escaping. I'll drive the getaway car," I joke.

"I might hold you to it one day," Tally says, and I'm not sure if she's serious or not. I guess we'll find out in the future. Taking another scone with me, I head out the back door and come around the front. I'm heading toward the big barn where all the hustle and bustle is. Today, we have four families coming in for vacations. One day, I think we're really going to have to expand out farther on the property and put more cabins up. The way things book up around here, it's a wonder people keep trying to book.

My father has done a great job at building this place into what it is. I'm not sure I'd ever want to leave. This is my home, and it's where I intend for my kids to grow up. Mirella's question really did solidify that. That is what I want in my future. Possibly buying a ranch of my own wouldn't be such a terrible idea either. It's not like I can raise my kids in the homestead here. We would all outgrow this place fast.

"Hello, Sleeping Beauty," Hudson mocks as I step inside.

"Shut up. It's not like you haven't slept in before." I shake my head and go straight for Dad's office door. After texting Mirella, I wanted to run a few things by Dad, and maybe he might be willing to help.

"Be warned. He's in a foul mood today. Not sure why, though," Hudson says.

Ignoring him, I knock. The grunt from inside tells me the same story.

"Hey, Dad," I say as I enter.

"You're late," he blurts out in his disappointed tone, one all of us are all too familiar with. We tend to overlook it. "If that girl is the cause of this, I think you should stop spending time there or at least stop the late nights."

I can't hold in the eruption of laughter that bursts from me. "You're kidding me, right? After everything with Delilah, you're still trying to run our love lives. Dad, you can't do that. It's not like I slack off or anything, or like you haven't started a little later in the day before. Plus, it's only nine in the morning. It's not lunchtime. Just stop." I groan, but I'm not willing to let him speak to me as though I'm still sixteen years old.

Dad drops his pen and then rests his hands on his face and rubs it. He finally looks in my direction. He's tired. His eyes tell a story of their own. He even looks sad. I take a seat in front of his desk and wait. William Reily has never been a man of feelings. None of us kids have ever seen him cry, other than when Mom died. That was it.

"I'm sorry, Harley. I'm stressed, and you were the target today. Thanks for reminding me to pull my head in. I can always count on you and Delilah to tell me to wake up in a not-so-subtle way." He sighs and leans back into his chair. He's a tall man, and boy, can he work with a horse.

I chuckle. "That's what we're here for. What's going on, Dad?"

"It's just the preparation for this fundraising fair and getting everything organized. I might need to hire someone to do the planning and make arrangements for me because with everything around here, I just can't do it all like I once did," he admits, and it's weird for him to openly acknowledge that.

Then, it hits me. "I might have someone who could possibly help with the organization of things. Give her a good idea of what you want, and she and I could do it."

"Don't you have your hands full with that horse?"

"I can work with her still at different times, and in those times, Mirella can take care of things. Even the girls could help her since they all pitch in some for this event." I'm excited at the thought of seeing Mirella more, and being able to get to know her better, and for her to meet my family.

Dad rubs the stubble on his chin, which is now a mixture of colors, but mostly gray. "Is this the girl living with Dotty at the moment? Would she be allowed to work for us if she's helping Dotty over there?"

"I can talk to her and see if it's something she's interested in doing, and maybe she can come to some arrangement with Dotty. From what Mirella has told me, she is working there to cover her rent and food."

"Okay, talk to her and let me know as soon as possible."

"Thanks, Dad." I go to get up and stop. "Hey, Dad, I've been wondering... why do you and Dotty not get along?"

"That's none of your concern." The muscle in his jaw ticks.

"I just find it odd that she dislikes us, and we haven't had anything to do with her, and when we try to be nice to her, we're met with animosity."

Dad turns back to his books and computer screen, basically his way of ending the conversation. Then, he says, "It's not you she dislikes."

"So, it's you. Did she and Mom get along? And did something happen after Mom died?" I continue to probe.

"Harley, stop asking questions and get to work," Dad snaps, the gruffness in his words stopping me short.

I'm silent as I sit and watch him a moment. "I'm going to find out one way or another, and I'd rather hear it from you, my father, instead of finding out through other means. Do you think we like to be treated like we've done something wrong, even though we've had nothing to do with that lady? Dad, what happened that's so terrible that we can't know?" I keep digging that hole. I'm fully invested in finding out why they hate each other. It has to be something to do with Mom. Though, now that I think about it, Dotty didn't really talk to Mom either.

"Get out." Anger pours off him, and those two words slice right through me.

"Fine, but this isn't over," I snap, rising from my seat, and I storm out the door. Hudson waits there with a smug look on his face.

"See? I told you he was in a mood," he chortles.

"No, he was fine until I started asking questions about Dotty," I say under my breath as I stride past him, out through the doors, marching down to the smaller stable. I have work to do, and I can't be around a man who thinks it's okay to keep secrets and let his kids continually get treated like garbage even though we've done nothing wrong to this woman.

Hudson stops and then runs to catch up. "Why would you ask about her? We all know that he's not going to give up anything on her."

"That's not the point. I've gone there so many times to see Mirella, and she's just so rude. Why should we be treated that way?" It's pathetic the way it's all of a sudden gotten to me, but Dad's reaction has made me question things even more. In the past, I've been happy to let things go, just thinking they disliked each other for some reason, but deep down, I really think there's more to it.

Hudson claps me on the shoulder. "Bro, is there even a point to this annoyance? I mean, it's been this way between our families for as long as I can recall, and being the oldest, I would have remembered if anything major happened between us, surely."

"I don't know. I think there's more, and they're not saying anything. Anyway, I have some work to do."

"Don't forget we have to go and gather some firewood for Friday night," he says.

"Yeah, just let me know when." I don't stop

walking. I go right inside the small barn and stop, glancing around. Then, I stop when I see a figure in a hoodie by the horse's pen gate. "Hey, be careful. She's not very tame at the moment."

The person jumps and turns in my direction. It's Mirella.

Chapter 13

Mirella

I WASN'T EXPECTING ANYONE TO come down here. Dotty and I had swapped some harsh words this morning, and instead of discussing it like an adult, I hightailed it out of there. It's possibly the only thing I'm good at these days — running when things get tough. Not that working for Dotty is tough. It was more like she snapped. She started throwing accusations at me about Harley and saying he only wants me for one thing. That he's not a very nice person. This all could have come about because I mentioned going to do some work for Harley's family to bring in some kind of income, but I said I'd still be able to help her as well.

I can't help but wonder if she's hanging onto

the past, the stuff with Olive, a little too tightly. What if there's a roadblock, and she is unable to move forward?

"Mirella!" Harley exclaims and rushes to me. He wraps his arms around my waist, his grip firm and welcome. I've needed his embrace. I wanted to be near him but didn't know how to find him. I knew he'd be working the horses but then realized I had no idea what horses or where. So, I saw this barn and was only going to hide out here for a little while, but the horse caught me off-guard. Once again, I'm on his property. I'll never learn. It was him that I was hoping to find, and I would have texted him and asked him to come down here if he wasn't here already.

He releases me and then looks me up and down, possibly to make sure that I am visibly okay.

"Sorry. I know I shouldn't be here," I say. "I didn't think this place was in use. It's quite old-looking." I swipe the hair out of my face and take him in. Always in jeans and a tee—a uniform I've come to love, especially on him.

"It's okay. Are you alright? You appear a little flustered," he says, and I feel it.

I nod. "I'll be okay. It's nothing I haven't dealt with before. Still hurts, though, to have someone think I'm doing the wrong thing when that isn't the case." My words crack with emotions caught in my throat. Clearing them away, I continue,

"She is a beautiful horse." I gesture to the chestnut-colored horse that is skittering around the pen. She was fine a moment ago while it was just me, but the moment Harley walked in, her mood changed.

"I'm training her. She doesn't seem to be settling, though. Nothing I do is working." He rubs his hand behind his neck, strides over to the pen gate, and watches her.

I follow. "She came over to me before you got here and even let me pat her nose," I offer. He turns to face me, his eyes wide.

"This horse let you pat her?"

I nod.

"She didn't try to bite you?"

I shake my head.

"It must be me, then. She could have been abused by men, and it's made her uncomfortable with me. It makes sense." He moves away to a cupboard. When he's gone, the horse comes up to me again and presses her nose against my outstretched hand.

"See?" I say gently, hoping Harley will hear me. "You're a big softy, aren't you?" As scary as these animals are, I'm drawn to her. She's special in her own way—not that I'd go jump on her back anytime soon. Any sudden movements would most likely startle her.

"There you go," Harley gushes, then says, "Maybe you can help me train her?"

"Nope, I'm no horse trainer. I'm just a city girl who's afraid of big animals. I wanted to talk to you about your job offer with the cleaning. I think I could really use the cash to help me get a better kickstart at a new life." I snap my mouth shut. I've said too much. I don't miss Harley's facial expression hardening slightly.

"You weren't hurt, were you?" he asks. A swell in my chest lifts the heaviness that has been weighing me down since the incident with Dotty this morning. I'm so grateful to her for all her help, and I'm not running out on her, but I can't have her mothering me like my own did. It's another reason why leaving that life behind was better for me.

I hold up my arms. "No, not hurt in that way. I don't want to discuss it right now."

"Urgh, what is it with people and keeping secrets or not wanting to talk about things? I'm so sick of it." He growls and kicks at the dirt on the ground. A puff of dust floats off in the small breeze.

Harley walks out into a round enclosure. Dotty has one set up to train her mustang. His outburst makes me wonder what he's talking about. Who else is keeping secrets? Of course his father is, but he doesn't know that. He just assumes that Dotty hates all his family.

I follow him out and stand by the gate. "What are you talking about? I am allowed to keep some things to myself. I hardly know you. You get that, right?"

He snorts. "You hardly know me, but you're happy to kiss and make out with me. Yeah, okay, that's fair."

I see red. It's as though a volcano has erupted within me. I storm up to him and shove him in the chest. "How dare you! You know nothing about me, and I'm sorry to have felt drawn to you and even liked you. Screw you, Harley. I'm not here to be spoken to like that." Turning on my heel, I slip through the fence and take off running back down the dirt road. I don't stop until I hit the property boundary where the cottage is. I take one glance over my shoulder before slipping through yet another fence. I'm becoming good at this.

Instead of heading back down to Dotty's house, I go in the opposite direction and toward the back of Dotty's property. Back here, it's mostly thick forest as I think Dotty hasn't been able to maintain it. I don't want to deal with Dotty or Harley. He didn't even come after me. I'm not here to be treated like that by anyone. We shared a few special moments, but the way he threw them back in my face tells me they meant very little to him. Why would someone do that? Be so hurtful toward someone else?

One day, I'll tell him about my family, but when it comes to them, I'd rather not. I'm not ready to talk about them to anyone. Not even Dotty knows my full story.

When I've gone far enough, I swap my jog for a slow walk. I'm not a runner by any means, and today has proven that. I huff out some large breaths and inhale deep ones to fill my lungs. I've managed to head into the thick trees. It's shady and away from everyone.

I look around. The forest area is beautiful, full of greenery. Even some wild yellow and white flowers litter the ground in spots. As I continue deeper into the woods, I come across a small clearing that's got some sun and a little shade from the trees. This looks like the perfect spot to take a seat, which I do by a thick-trunked tree. Perfect.

I reach around and retrieve the journal I have tucked into the back of my jeans. I was planning to read it while in that old barn, but that didn't turn out how I'd wanted. It was a trainwreck. I've probably alienated the one friend I had around here. I know it's about two hours to the nearest town, and that's a little too far for me to walk. Hiding out for a little bit won't hurt anyone and is a better option.

Today, William and I told our parents. I was more than shocked when I met William at the cottage, and he even had a golden engagement ring with a simple, round-cut diamond. He was prepared for this to work—determined, more like it.

I thanked him and gave him a small kiss on the lips. I mean, I've got to start loving this man, and each tiny step, kiss, and touch will all make that happen. Who doesn't love to feel loved? To feel as though you're cared about by someone other than your immediate family.

I want that. Unconditional love. I thought Ryan was the person to give that to me, and I was wrong. Someone who has shown an ounce of care is William. I have to give him the chance he deserves, and I will.

We stopped at my house first. My mom and dad were shocked yet thrilled. Dotty, not so much. She stood behind them. With my stomach in a knot of nerves, I held my breath, hoping that she wouldn't blurt out my problem and reveal that William and I are kind of scamming our families—mostly mine, though. But they couldn't be happier.

When William mentioned that we wanted the wedding to happen sooner rather than later, meaning in two weeks, they were silent and glanced between us. Mom even glanced at my stomach. William squeezed my hand, assuring me silently things would be okay.

They were okay. Mom said we'd get right to work and plan something small but beautiful. I couldn't be happier that she's on board. William's parents didn't care at all. They've been waiting for this announcement for a long time. His mom called mine, and the planning is now underway. I'm not sure I'll get much of a say in the event itself, but that's okay because, right now, I have to concentrate on not giving away my pregnancy. I've heard people can get really sick and some don't. I haven't hit the sickness stage yet, but I'm already tired, which is *another sign. Add in the sore boobs, and we're all set for now.*

William's father offered the cottage to us as our first little space. I would never say no. We graciously accepted, and while our mothers planned the wedding, we organized our future home. I have loved this cottage for as long as I can remember. I'll never forget watching William work endlessly on this place. It had already been here a long time and needed lots of work and repairs, which he took care of. Now it's a beautiful little place to start a family.

I should be excited for my wedding day, but the joy I should have is being washed away by Dotty and her coldness. After we'd announced our engagement to the families, William had to go back and get some work done for the day. I, on the other hand, went to speak to Dotty.

Our conversation wasn't a nice one. In fact, she went so far as to call me a name I won't write here. She's right, though. I did the wrong thing, and now William and I are doing something we probably would never have done if it wasn't for my stupidity.

"You have ruined everything for me. I have always loved William." Her words were like a dagger to my heart. She actually loves him. He's never felt the same for her as she has for him. I don't know how to fix this. Will we ever move past this?

More next time,

Olive

Chapter 14

Harley

WHAT A FREAKIN' DAY. I storm into the kitchen, throwing my hat on the counter. "What's wrong with you?" Sybil demands from behind me.

I whirl around and clutch at my chest. "Gee, you gave me a fright. Don't you know it's not nice to scare people? And for the record, nothing is wrong."

Rolling her eyes, she nods. "Whatever you say. You've been in a mood since you came back from training that horse. What happened down there? Did she bite you?" she jokes, clearly not reading the signs that I'm not interested in talking with her.

"Oh, go away, Sybil. I'm not in the mood for this."

"And there it is—the cranky Harley we've heard about all day." She cheers and stands from the seat she was occupying at the dining room table.

I open my mouth to retort but am cut off when a thunderous knock blasts the front door.

"I wonder who that is?" I ask. The sun is gone for the day, and it's time to settle down for the night, yet someone's found it necessary to go nuts at our front door.

Before I can get to it, Dad opens the door. "What do you want?" he almost growls as his body becomes rigid.

"Where is she?" Dotty's voice is shrill as it carries down the hallway. Sybil and I glance at each other, wide-eyed. There has never been a time when Dotty has come onto our property. Not even when we had those bushfires years ago. She kept her property safe and wouldn't help us, even though we almost lost everything.

"Where is who?" Dad retorts coldly.

Slowly, Sybil and I make our way to the front door.

"Where is Mirella?" Dotty's worried yet fiery gaze lands on me, and she takes a step in my direction.

Dad and Sybil turn to me, awaiting my answer. My stomach plummets and crashes to the floor. Anxiety crawls into its place. "I don't know. I haven't seen her since this morning."

"This morning?" Dad asks, his jaw ticking away. His angry face is plastered on. This is the side of Dad no one likes to see.

"She was down at the training barn earlier, and we had a little argument since I was already in a mood because of you, and then she ran off in the direction of Mom's cottage. I let her go. I wasn't in the right frame of mind to chase her and clear things up. I was going to call her tonight." The words rush from me, but the nerves cause my body to tremble. Where is Mirella?

Dotty runs her hands over her head, and tears sit in her eyes. "Can you help me find her please? I would never normally impose, but I am now. I won't ask for anything again."

Before she can continue with her speech, I head out the door and go right for the barn.

"Where are you going?" Dad calls from the front porch with Dotty walking toward her car.

"I'm going to look for her out near Mom's cottage, and maybe farther out, and possibly over on Dotty's side. I need to find her." Fear claws through me. If only I'd gotten over myself this morning and gone after her. What kind of person does that make me?

I shouldn't have said what I did, and now no one knows where she is or if she's hurt. Thankfully, Chester is still saddled up as I was going to come back down after I'd had some water and brush him down.

I climb up into the saddle and take off from the barn with Hudson calling out, "Hey, where are you going in such a hurry?"

Ignoring him, I keep going. I will find her. I hope she's not injured. The memory of Mom comes flashing back into my mind. Shaking my head, I attempt to clear it away. What if Mirella is hurt and can't get help? This is all my fault. I was stupid and should have messaged her or gone after her.

I ride along until I get to the cottage, which is pitch black. After jumping off Chester, I stop at the bottom of the few steps leading to the front door of Mom's sanctuary—a place I've not been inside for years. I pull my phone from my pocket and press Mirella's name on my list. I wait anxiously, and then the line rings. In the distance, I hear a phone ringing. Following the sound, I walk along the fence line, past the cottage, and finally, I come to a stop. Then, I see it—a phone. It's clearly hers.

I slip through to Dotty's side of the fence line and pick it up. "Where are you?" I scan the area around me, looking for some kind of movement. She wouldn't leave her phone here. Something's happened.

"Mirella!" I call as loudly as my voice will go. It echoes into the night. Farther up the road is thick, dense bushland on Dotty's property. What if she's gotten lost?

Taking off toward the forest, I call her name again and again. Still no response. Breathless and panicked sensations don't go well together. I become lightheaded as I reach the edge of the thick trees and make my way in, again calling her name, only to be met by silence.

I can't and won't stop until I find her. "Please be okay. I need her to be okay," I plead with whoever might be listening, maybe even Mom. I'm not a believer in ghosts, angels, or anything like that, but I need something right now.

Up ahead, a figure catches the corner of my eye—a body in a clearing, slumped over against a tree trunk. "No," I breathe and take off running, my heart in my throat with each step I take.

Getting closer, I notice the clothing, the black tee and jeans that Mirella was wearing this morning, and the scene before me is like in my nightmares. Only, this time, it's not my mother on the ground in front of me. It's Mirella.

"No, not again," I sob, dropping to my knees beside her, my heart breaking all over again.

Chapter 15

Mirella

I STARTLE AWAKE AT SOMEONE grabbing my hand. Snatching it back, I say, "What the heck?" I blink a few times for my blurry eyes to clear.

"Oh, my goodness. You're okay." Harley's broken words cause my stomach to tighten with worry. What is he doing out here? And when did it get so dark? After a short moment, I realize now why he might be panicked. It's night, and I guess no one has heard from me. I must have fallen asleep while reading the journal.

Harley rolls back onto his butt and places his face in his hands, resting his elbows on his knees. His almost silent sobs tear right through me like a wild storm. I slowly shuffle closer to him, placing my arm over his shoulder.

"Harley, what's wrong?" I ask, confused by his reaction.

He doesn't speak. His shoulders shake under my touch, and I don't know what to do. I've never seen a man break down like this. The look of fear mixed with relief that I saw on his face the moment I met his eyes is one I'll never forget.

My heart beats double time, and I scan the ground for the diary. When I see it, I sigh. I'll pick it up once I can figure out what's wrong with Harley. He's shaken up, and the worry rippling through me is something I can't push aside.

"Harley, can you talk to me please? I'm worried," I try again, this time moving my face to his and resting my forehead against the side of his head, which is still buried in his hands. I press my lips to his warm, prickly cheek and sit with him, waiting. "I'm all right, Harley. You're all right. We are good," I assure him, rubbing my hand over his back. "Take a breath," I say gently.

After a while, his body stops trembling, and he settles. We sit in silence, and I wait for him to be ready. A phone rings, startling both of us. It's my phone, but it's somehow found its way into Harley's pocket. *That's strange.* He digs in and hands it over to me, remaining silent.

"Hello?" I say after answering Dotty's call.

"Oh, my goodness, are you okay?" She sighs, the relief evident in her rushed words.

Before answering, I pause a moment and recall our conversation this morning and then me running away. I sigh. "Uh, yeah, I am. Sorry." I rub my stiff neck and take in Harley, who is now finally looking up at me. His eyes are red, and his face is blotchy.

"Mirella, you've been missing all day. I even went over to Harley's house, and he rode off on a horse, and now I don't know where he is." I'm not sure if Dotty's angry or not. Her tone keeps changing.

Guilt crashes into me. "I'm so sorry, Dotty. I'll be home soon. Harley is with me. We will be back shortly," I assure her, and I end the call and make a move to get up. As I do, I grab the journal and tuck it back into my jeans. Harley moves slowly while he gets up and dusts himself off, almost like he's injured.

"Harley, what's going on? Please talk to me." Stepping closer, I take his hand, pulling him against me.

"I'm sorry about that," he says in barely a whisper. He's unable to meet my eyes.

"Something is going on, and I wish you would tell me what," I urge, squeezing his hand.

He shakes his head. "Seeing you there, on the ground..." He stops and takes a shaky breath. "It brought back a painful memory. One I've never gotten over." Clearing his throat, he pulls me against his chest and inhales deeply.

"Does it have to do with your mom?" I take a random guess because his reaction was very deep. Seeing him so vulnerable and raw like that has shaken me.

He nods. "Yeah. It's also a part of the reason I won't go in the cottage. I found my mom passed out on the floor there. I took her back home, and she only lived another day. I've never fully healed from the experience of seeing my mom on the floor, unmoving and unresponsive. It broke me." Tears stream down his face as he relays his private story to me.

"I am so sorry, Harley. That must have been so hard for you." I wrap my arms around his waist and pull him against me, needing to comfort him and give him the care and support that he needs. "I'm sorry I scared you today. I got caught up reading a book and just fell asleep."

"You lost your phone as well. Not sure if you noticed that or not," Harley says and takes a step back, putting a bit of distance between us.

"Oh no, I didn't realize. It must have fallen out when I was running. I was pretty annoyed at you and Dotty and needed some time away from everything." I hang my head and kick my sneaker over a patch of long grass.

Harley's hand comes under my chin, tilting it

up until our eyes meet. The connection, the desire between us is like the beginning of a bonfire, and it's only a matter of time before the sparks combust into flames. I wouldn't push him away.

"I am so sorry for how I spoke to you this morning. I was already in a bad mood because of my father, but that's no excuse for how I treated you. I should know better. My mother always told me to never leave an argument hanging for too long or it could become too late to fix it."

"Your mother was a smart woman." I shyly smile. His hand moves to cup my cheek, and I close my eyes as I soak up his touch and this moment—a moment any girl would dream of. We're under the dark of night, the stars surrounding us, and it's just us again. I've found another moment with a man who seems to be stealing my heart, body, and soul.

"Yes, she was," he says softly and glides his fingertips over my cheek. I think it's time we get you back so Dotty can relax. She has never been at our place. In my whole life, she has not set foot there once. You must be important to her." He drops his hand and then wraps his arm around my waist, and I do the same with him.

"I'm glad you came looking for me."

"I couldn't not. I needed to find you, and after this morning, I needed to apologize for what I'd said. I'm just so sick of secrets. Dad is keeping something from me. I know it. And then you didn't want to talk about things, and it all got to me. I snapped. I'm not proud of the way I handled things, and then to hear you'd been missing since I last saw you... I'd never been more scared in my life." He clears the tightness from his throat and keeps me close as we walk out of the forest. "I'll walk you home."

"I'd like that." I look ahead to the dirt road. We still have a long way to walk, and maybe, since he's shared something personal with me, it's my turn to give him a little. Before I manage to organize the words in my head, I blurt out, "I ran away from home, and I'm basically hiding out here at Dotty's. A friend helped me run away, and I haven't had any contact with my parents since I left." I bite my lip as I wait for Harley's response.

"I'm not entirely sure what to say," he replies with a small chuckle. "I mean, I knew there was obviously something going on with your family, but wow. Why did you run away?"

I take a deep breath and say, "Because my parents were forcing me to marry someone who was pretty much the playboy of New York and was with a different woman every other day. It was a business marriage."

Harley stops and turns to me, releasing his grip on my waist. "Is that even legal?" His usually relaxed and happy demeanor has suddenly transformed into something stone cold.

I choke out a laugh. "It's not in my book. They were only doing it for money. My parents are actually pretty wealthy. When I left, I turned my back on all of that. I don't want any of their money, especially if it means I have to marry that vile man. I'd be the unhappiest newlywed, and it would probably be over within a month, if not days. There was no way I was letting that man lie in a bed with me." I grit my teeth together at the thought of him claiming me as another one of his trophies.

He clears his throat, then says, "What was in it for him? If it was for the money, but your parents are rich, then why was it happening at all? Sorry if that's too forward. If you don't want to answer, that's fine."

I smile, actually finding it so much easier to talk to him. "For him, it was to gain access to his part of his father's fortune that he receives only when he gets married and has at least one child. Though, I'm pretty sure he's probably got a secret child out there somewhere."

"Wow, that's really a thing? I thought that's something that only happens in the movies." He chuckles.

"Yep, it happens in real life. My parents wanted his family's business name on their sponsor list for future events they have coming up, so it was a win-win for both sides—just not me." I finish, and he remains silent, but it's comfortable, as though some of the weight I've been carrying on my shoulders has lifted a bit.

We keep walking, our shoes crunching on the dirt. With a shake of his head, he reaches for my hand. "If I ever see this man, or even your parents, I might lose my mind."

I quickly glance over at him. His jaw is set and rigid. He's not joking. Harley is a protector, and I admire him deeply for that. Not everyone has the instinct to keep others safe. My parents surely don't.

"Don't worry, I don't think they'll ever think to look this far out of town. I am a city girl, remember? And I was raised a certain way—to enjoy the finer things in life. They think I'll stick to that, so I did something completely different, and now I'm out here."

"Yeah, now you're shoveling poop instead of going on shopping sprees. How did you end up with Dotty?"

I shrug. "The guy who helped me arranged it. I simply went along with it." We walk in silence for a beat before I say, "I do enjoy it out here, and I'm just glad that I've made at least one or two friends, if you include Dotty."

He bumps my shoulder playfully. "Don't worry. After you meet my sisters, you'll have plenty more friends. Oh, the joys of coming from a big family." He chuckles.

"I wish I came from one, because then I'd be invisible to my parents, and I wouldn't need to worry about this. I probably wouldn't have needed to run away, because the focus would be on another sibling," I respond dryly.

"Don't get me wrong. Having a big family is good and bad. Sometimes, having the focus on a sibling can be a good thing, but other times, you can feel invisible when you need the attention. Everyone has their own opinions, and someone gets offended over something another one said." He laughs, and it brings me joy hearing it after his breakdown earlier. I don't want to ever be the cause of that anguish again.

We finally arrive back at Dotty's, and she's waiting on the back porch, pacing the length of it until she sees us coming down the road. After racing down the few stairs, she rushes up to meet us.

"You silly girl. Why did you do that to me?" Her voice cracks, and I know she's not being nasty. It's how she shows she cares. Everyone responds differently. She gives me a quick hug and then holds me at arm's length, her eyes scanning over me.

"I'm sorry. I fell asleep under a tree, and I lost track of the time. Harley found me and my phone that had fallen from my pocket this morning." I'm cut off when a truck comes roaring up Dotty's dirt driveway, kicking up dust in its path.

A tall, burly-looking man jumps from the driver's side of the car and strides toward the three of us, a young woman following a few steps behind him. "Is this her?" he asks in a deep voice, and he turns his gaze on Dotty and then on Harley.

"Yeah, Dad, it is. I found her in the forest at the back of Dotty's property," Harley confirms. "Dad, this is Mirella. Mirella, this is my dad, William."

"Nice to meet you." I extend my hand to shake, which he does. "I'm sorry to have caused a fuss."

"Sometimes a little fuss is needed around here," the dark-haired girl who is standing behind William says in a mocking tone, glaring between Dotty and William.

"And this is one of my sisters, Sybil. Sybil, Mirella."

"Nice to meet you," she gushes, and instead of offering a handshake, she comes right in for a hug, almost pushing Harley out of the way. William sighs and rubs his head, exactly what Harley does as well. Sybil steps back, and the circle becomes quiet.

"Thanks for all of your help," Dotty says softly and even gives William a tiny smile. Could this be a step in the right direction for the families to possibly mend things?

"We're glad she's okay," William says and shifts his stance, averting his gaze. "Where did you leave Chester?" he asks Harley.

"Just up at the cottage. I'll go get him and be home shortly," he responds, and with that, William turns to leave.

"It was nice to meet you, Mirella. I hope this won't be the last time either." Sybil winks, and I know I like her right away.

"Yeah, you, too. I'm sure I'll see you again," I say with a small nod.

Dotty takes my arm. "I'm going inside. I'll give you a moment. Thanks again for finding her, Harley. Mirella, if you want to go and do some work for Harley's family, you're more than welcome. I would still expect you to complete your work here, though."

I step forward and give her a quick hug. "Thank you. I'll always be here to help you because you've helped me." When I release her, she doesn't say anything but turns and heads back up the stairs and in through the back door.

"Well, that was an eventful moment," Harley jokes. "And Dad and Dotty even spoke — that's a miracle. The first time in so long that it's been civil. They're always snarky with each other."

"Thanks for sharing your personal story with me. It made it easier for me to open up to you and share my story," I say.

Harley takes my face in his hands, and before I can say any more, his mouth is on mine. The emotions that have passed between us make the kiss deeper. I want him. He makes me feel alive. The power within one move and connection is just... wow. Breathtaking and spectacular.

He can hold me and shower me in kisses for as long as he wants. I'm not going anywhere anytime soon.

Chapter 16

Harley

"HAVE YOU BOYS COLLECTED THE firewood for tonight?" Dad asks as he comes into the kitchen.

Hudson and I are finishing off our breakfasts of bacon and eggs that Mabel has cooked up for everyone. They're all excited because Delilah will be home around lunchtime, which means Olive will be as well, so the level of excitement around the house today is off the charts.

"It's first up this morning," Hudson replies with a mouthful of toast.

Odette smacks his arm. "Don't talk with your mouth full," she says, pointing at his mouth.

Laughter erupts around the room. It's Odette's job to keep us all in check sometimes, and she's good at it and doesn't hold back.

"Okay," Dad says as he fills his plate with food and comes to sit down. Since the other night, when Mirella disappeared and Dotty came and asked for help, something within my dad has changed. His usual stone-cold expression has somewhat subsided. It still shows its face every now and then, but not as much. "Harley, have you asked Mirella for that help? I'm guessing it was her that you were referring to when you said you had someone in mind."

"I haven't had a chance. Things have been crazy around here. I'll pop over after I help out with the firewood this morning." I chomp on another piece of toast and rest back in my chair, stretching out my now full stomach. "Thanks for breakfast, Mabel," I offer as she flits back into the room after being gone a moment.

"Yeah, it's been nice not slaving away in the kitchen for once," Tally jokes, sitting beside me. Even her cranky mood has vanished—for now. I'm forever guessing Tally's mood, but I'm thankful everyone is on the same frequency today.

"Can you get Mirella to come by at some point so I can talk to her as well after you talk with her please?" Dad asks.

I almost choke on my toast at the word please. Something has definitely switched around in the universe. Have we somehow managed to open up a new universe, and this dad isn't the one from here?

I don't voice my shock, but act cool. "Sure, not a problem. She still has to say yes yet, but I think it'll be okay."

"I like her," Sybil says, entering the kitchen without missing a beat of the conversation. I swear, her hearing is something mythical. No one should be able to pick up what she does sometimes.

"That's good to know," I say and watch as Sybil fills her plate and comes to sit beside me.

"You two will be great together. I have no doubt." She puts some bacon in her mouth and chomps down.

"Gee, thanks," I respond dryly, wanting to disappear from this conversation. Mirella has been a hot topic these past few mornings since Sybil and Dad have now met her.

My phone chimes, and everyone's eyes turn on me as I pull the cell out of my back pocket. When I glance up, I say, "What?"

"Who is it from?" Sybil asks.

Dropping my eyes to the screen, I answer, "It's Mirella. What's the big deal?"

"Oh, okay. I thought it might have been Delilah giving us an update or something." Everyone goes back to what they were doing, and I open my message.

Mirella: *Hey, how are things this morning? I remember you said your other sister comes back today. Are we still on for lunchtime at the cottage?*

"Check out that cheesy grin," Mabel teases.

"Oh, grow up." I attempt to wipe the smile off my face, but I can't. This is the kind of effect that Mirella has on me.

I type a quick reply.

Harley: *Yep, cottage at lunchtime. I think my family has been swapped out for aliens. My dad is being nice, and everyone is getting along. That might change the moment Delilah arrives, and everyone wants to spend time with Olive. Someone needs to have another baby in this house to keep everyone occupied, and it's not going to be me.*

Mirella: *I'll be there. I get the baby thing. Babies and little kids have some kind of magical power. The way they can turn situations around... it's just wow. I'm nowhere near ready for a baby. They are so much work, and I'm still working on my family problems.*

Harley: *Don't worry. It'll all work out, but there will have to come a day where you contact your parents and just talk to them.*

Mirella: *I swear, I just choked on my laughter. Gee, you're funny, especially if you think my family is going to listen to anything I have to say. Even though I'm of age and an adult, they don't see that. To them, I'm a puppet on a string they can manipulate how they see fit.*

I love how she's being more open with me about her family situation. It's not ideal, but I get it.

"Who you messaging?" Odette asks from across the table.

My head comes up, and I grin at her. "Just a friend who is staying with Dotty."

"Dotty cranky?" Odette picks up on most things, and she's probably heard conversations around the house time and time again about Dotty.

I shake my head. "No, she's okay," I say gently.

Odette nods and then taps the table in the way that helps her cope with something, or it's one of her tics.

"Where's Devon this morning?" I ask, trying to take her mind off whatever is going through it.

Her head comes up. "Working," she states and goes back to eating her fruit. He'll be coming out to help get wood this morning. He's a good kid with a massive heart. He only wants to fit in with people around here.

I go back to messaging Mirella.

Harley: *I am sorry about your family and the way they think. I hope it'll get better one day, because surely you'd hate to shut your parents out completely for the rest of your life. I've lost a parent, and I know what that pain feels like. Even* *if you don't get along, don't let that hate for what they have been doing to you overshadow the fact that they are your family, and that if something happened to either one of them, you'd be there in a heartbeat to support each other. It's a natural instinct.*

Mirella: *That's true. One day, I'll reach out, but not right now. Things are still raw. I'm not ready to talk to them about it yet because they won't hear me. They're only seeing dollar signs at the moment.*

Harley: *Okay, I just wanted to put that out there for you. Change of subject—are you still coming to the bonfire tonight? The rest of my family are keen to meet you.*

Mirella: *Gee, that's not nerve-racking at all. You're basically throwing me into the lion's den. Are they going to tear me to pieces with all their questions?*

Harley: *Ha ha! If you don't want to answer any questions, then don't. Trust me, they all have thick skin. You might not be able to resist Odette, though. She's very blunt and is quite persistent when she wants answers to something.*

Mirella: *Ha ha! Thanks for letting me know. I better get downstairs, or Dotty will be back up here, pounding on my door. I'll see you at lunchtime.*

Harley: *See you then.*

Looking up, I realize Dad is gone, as is Hudson. "Dang it. I better get to work, then," I mutter to myself.

"It's okay to have a moment and chat with her. I mean, you give a lot of time and energy to this place. It's okay to have some time for you," Mabel says kindly as she collects the empty plate from in front of me.

"Thanks, Mabel. Not sure Dad sees things that way." I rise from my seat.

"True, but he saw you engrossed in your messaging, and he didn't get mad or tell you to put it away and get to work." She makes a great point, and I'm stumped as to why Dad didn't do that.

"He's been different since the other night when Dotty came around asking for help," I say slowly as I push my chair in.

Mabel nods. "I've noticed it, too. Maybe they were lovers back in the day. We have been neighbors with their family for years. Before Mom and Dad got married as well." She pauses a moment before continuing, "Do you think it's weird that we don't really know much of Mom and Dad's story from back then? Usually, parents share stories from their time as kids and maybe mention their own parents. We've heard about Dad's family a bit, but not Mom's. It makes me think, that's all."

I lean against the doorframe and watch as Mabel loads the dishwasher. "I've thought something similar. Do you think Mom kept anything from when she was a kid? Surely, Dad has a box or something of Mom's stuff. He wouldn't throw it out, would he?" I ask.

Mabel shrugs. "I don't know. If I was looking for answers, I'd probably start in the library. That place is full of Mom's special moments, photos, and memorabilia. Perhaps there's something hidden away in there." She stops rinsing off the dishes that wouldn't fit in the dishwasher and faces me. "Just remember that sometimes digging up the past isn't a good idea. Maybe there's a reason they have kept things from us. Just be careful and don't hurt those you love."

"Okay. Well, I better get to work." Heading out the door, I collect my hat from the hook by the door, putting it on my head as I mull over Mabel's last words. Could our parents' secrets really be that hurtful? What if they are, and I ruin what we have here as a family?

I can't risk hurting those I love. Any secrets are going to have to remain buried.

Chapter 17

Mirella

Today is the day. William and I are getting married, even though I'm scared for what the future holds and whether or not people are going to figure out he's not the father of this baby I'm carrying. Over the past two weeks, I've been swept up in wedding preparation. I had to show enthusiasm, or my mom would have been suspicious. Interestingly, she hasn't picked up on anything, because she's usually pretty good at figuring things out. Maybe the wedding stuff has kept her busy.

Thankfully, this baby hasn't made me too sick. I'm just really tired and experiencing the occasional wave of nausea. I need to go to the doctor for a checkup but haven't been able to. I don't want to alert my parents, and if I mention doctors, then they will want to know why. What if the baby isn't viable, and this wedding is all for nothing? These are the kinds of thoughts that invade my mind, especially late at night. I don't have Dotty to talk to anymore. When in the presence of others, especially Mom and Dad, she's kind, and we get along like we once did, but when we're alone, it's the complete opposite. She doesn't talk to me—doesn't even acknowledge me. I am heartbroken over this whole situation with us.

William and I have grown closer, and I'm really enjoying his company. When I told him about Dotty and how she's been acting, he comforted me and told me that I could talk to him anytime, that after the wedding it's going to be us till death do us part. He wants to be my best friend and husband. I could not have asked for a better man in my life. It's a happy and sad time.

I'm happy to have someone on my side who's there for me, even knowing what I've done and the consequences of that. William cares for me.

I'm sad because my relationship with my sister has fallen apart. I feel like I've lost her, and I don't know how to fix it. I could possibly cancel this whole wedding and come clean, but my feelings for William are changing daily. I could even grow to love him.

More soon,

Olive

I GRIN AT THE PAGE before me. Lying on my stomach on my bed with the journal on my pillow, I flip to the back of the pages and pull out the photo of a young William and Olive, her blonde hair pinned back and with a crown of small flowers weaved through it. There's no way I could tell they were faking their love in this moment. They appear to be the happiest couple ever in this image. The black-and-white tone makes this picture all the more beautiful. Their love must have grown and blossomed like a beautiful rose.

Why didn't Dotty forgive and forget? She had one sister, and now she's gone. Did they ever get a chance to sort things out? I'm guessing not, because her and William don't talk either, except for the other night when I was missing.

As I flip through the pages without reading them, I see that this journal jumps through the years, as though Olive only wrote in it when she remembered to. I flip to the last entry, and the date in it was about ten years ago, or just over. I won't read that just yet, but it's like this is her life in one book. Wow, I would have gotten tired of it and jumped from notebook to notebook. I wouldn't have been able to help myself.

I look at my watch and realize I'm going to be late to meet with Harley. Jumping up, I shove the pictures back in the journal and shove the journal under my pillow. Thankfully, Dotty respects my privacy and doesn't come in here unless invited.

I race out the back door and down the road. I catch Dotty working in the pen with her mustang. Going over, I say, "Maybe you should ask Delilah or Harley to have a go at training her. From what I have heard, Delilah is coming back today, and if you want, I can ask Harley to come over with her," I offer, already knowing what her answer will be. I want to try, though. To give her the chance to get to know her nieces and nephews.

Dotty comes to the fence and watches the mustang buck and throw its head about. "You know I'm not one to ask for help, don't you?"

I nod. "Yeah, I know that, which is why I would be asking, not you, and I'm kind of just getting your permission to do so," I say matter-of-factly, wanting to show respect and not step out of bounds by simply doing it without her knowledge and consent.

Dotty is silent a moment, and I admire the beautiful animal in front of us. She would be magical if she could be trained well, and the way Harley speaks of his sister and her skills in the ring, I thought I'd take a stab and ask her. The worst Dotty can do is say no, and Harley and his family won't get hurt because I wouldn't mention anything to them.

"All right, ask Harley and Delilah to come around at some point. I'm happy to pay them for their time as well. I'm no horse trainer, but I wanted to try before I gave anyone else a go. I'm stubborn like that," Dotty admits with a small laugh.

"I get that. You're a prideful woman. I understand. Perhaps it's time to let people in a bit more," I suggest. Things between us have been so much better since I ran away. She hasn't been cranky as much, and the scowl she used to have plastered on her sun-worn face seems to have disappeared. "I'll ask him when I see him. He has something he wants to discuss with me about a job, so I'll let you know when I get back. And don't worry, if I'm not going to be home by sundown, I'll message you."

"Thank you. Off you go, then," she says gently and then goes back to work with her mustang. She's determined, I'll give her that.

I take off at a run down the dirt road and don't stop until the cottage comes into view, then I slow to a walk. A white truck sits out in the paddock, and I spot Harley sitting on the front porch steps. His face lights up when he sees me, and he gets up. Slipping through the fence, I walk toward him.

"You're late." His smug tone tells me he's trying to get a rise out of me.

"I'm not late—just on time. I was reading and then got caught up with Dotty, and guess what?" We meet halfway, and when we get close, Harley leans in and presses his mouth gently to mine.

"Oh, that was unexpected," I say. The warmth in my cheeks spreads to my chest.

"It feels like forever since I've seen you. I hope that's okay."

"It's completely okay. A girl could get used to those kinds of greetings," I reply with a smug grin.

"Well, get used to it, then, because I plan to greet you that way every single time," he says confidently. Is this his way of basically committing to an *us?*

I raise my eyebrows. "Is this your way of propositioning me to be your girlfriend?"

"Only if that's what you want. I know we haven't known each other very long, but I can't help the way you make me feel." He steps closer and wraps one arm around my waist, the other cupping my cheek. He really knows how to make a girl feel special.

"I'll have to think on that," I reply in a whisper before pausing a moment and then grinning. "I'd like it very much. You make me feel heard, feel special, as though what I have to say matters."

"You do matter. So much." His mouth meets mine, and I'm lost in the moment. With each kiss, he mends a piece of my shattered heart. It was broken after years of neglect and unrequited love. I want this so much. I want to shout it from the hilltops. He makes my heart sing with joy, and my body becomes so alive and awake after each and every one of his spine-tingling kisses.

When we finally come up for air, we release each other and simply hold hands, then we walk back to the cottage steps. When we sit down, he asks, "So, before I stole your train of thought, you had something to tell me?"

"Yes, I asked Dotty if she would mind if you and Delilah came over to work with her mustang. She's having horrible luck with it. And she said yes."

"Are you playing a joke on me?" Harley asks, shock evident in his voice.

I laugh. "No, she said you and Delilah could come over and try to help her."

"Wow, I'm shocked and excited because that horse would be great to work with. Though, I already have one I'm working with, and she doesn't seem to like me, but she likes you, and so if I'm going to help you, you have to help me a little with my horse," he proposes.

My heart beats double-time, and I'm speechless. It's as if he hasn't heard anything I've said in the past. These horses are big and scary. I don't want to make visiting them a habit or ride around on one every day of the week. Butter was lovely, and I'd have a small ride on her again, but I'm not okay with anything more. "I'm not sure. I know nothing about horses."

"Don't worry. I'll be there with you every step of the way. I wouldn't let one harm you. I'll be right beside you," he assures me and squeezes my hand, which settles my nerves a little.

"Fine, but if anything goes wrong at all, I'm done. No more horses for me." I pound my fist on my knee as if solidifying my response.

"Excellent. Now, I have something else to discuss with you. How would you like to work with my dad to organize this fundraising fair we have? He's getting swamped and needs some help to mostly take over and just run things by him for approval. He'll take care of the guest list, but maybe we could look into inviting some big businesses that have helped support us in the past. I know Sebastian is trying to bring in his team's support, too, and a few other Formula One teams have put their hands up to help. So, what do you think?"

It's a mountain of words for me to sort through. He wants me to help his dad. *His dad.*

"Just so I heard you right, you want me to help your dad?"

"Yes, he needs help, and it's very rare for him to admit that. Do you think you could do it?"

I shrug. "Maybe. I don't know. I'd need to talk to him about things."

Harley jumps up. "Let's go, then. It's the bonfire tonight, and we're preparing for that. How about you spend some time talking things through with Dad, and I'll do things to set up, and then I'll drop you home after we've spent some time around the fire?"

"Sounds good. I'll send Dotty a message and let her know." After pulling my cell from the back pocket of my jeans, I send her a quick message.

Mirella: *Will be home late tonight—going to the bonfire at Harley's. Also, he said he and Delilah will come help with Black Beauty.*

I've decided that's going to be her name now. It suits her.

"Done."

"Let's get going. We've got things to do, and I'm so glad you'll get to meet the rest of the family today. I know they're all keen to meet you, and I want to show you our library. It was one of Mom's favorite spots. She would be sitting in there either writing or reading, and Delilah was always her shadow. You'll love little Olive—that's Delilah's daughter. She wins over everyone's heart. Just if Tally comes across as angry or something, don't take it to heart. She's just like that, so it's not you. She's dealing with her own demons. Come on." He finally takes a breath after talking a mile a minute and takes my hand, leading me to the truck's passenger seat. I climb in, then he does.

After a moment, he pulls up outside what I think is the homestead—a beautiful white home with all the perfect country-style finishes, including hanging pot plants and colorful flower bushes surrounding the porch. I'm speechless. It's big and open. Not what I imagined at all. Though, I shouldn't have expected anything less when I think about the work they do here and how busy it must be.

"Welcome to my humble abode." Harley's grin is wide and proud.

"It's stunning." I climb out of the truck and soak in the scenery. I can see now why Harley is always busy. This place is crawling with people. The workers are in light-blue shirts, some are in the pens with people who I'm guessing are clients or vacationers. Then, there are people in a group watching a reptile show as the man holds a lizard of some sort.

"So nice of you to meet me!" a voice calls, and I whirl toward it. It's the blonde woman I met the day I took off on Black Beauty. She's come out of the house, a baby girl on her hip, with a trail of people following her—one of which steals the baby.

"Dee, what the heck? You weren't meant to be here until later." Harley races off and scoops her up in a brotherly hug. He puts her down and then tries to steal the baby. Sybil keeps her. It still doesn't stop him from smothering the baby in kisses.

"Sebastian got us an earlier flight, which is good. He's going to come when he has a mid-season break. Right now, their races are back-to-back for three weeks. I'm just glad to be back home and away from the spotlight." She sighs and then spots me. "Oh, hello. It's you." She points in my direction.

I give a wave and smile. "Hey again." I kind of want to run away and hide because it's all so much with everyone at once.

"Well, I'm glad you're all together. This is Mirella. She's staying over at Dotty's. Mirella, this is my family, minus Dad." Harley starts pointing people out. "Sybil you've already met, but this is Delilah, Mabel, Hudson, Tally — or Talulla — and Odette, and this little cutie is Olive." He gushes when he addresses the baby. It's adorable to watch.

They all rush in with their, "Nice to meet you," greetings, and I think Delilah even says, "Finally." I can't keep up with them, but they all come down and greet me either with a handshake or a hug. Odette dances around a little and gives me a wave. I love her free-spirited personality.

When Sybil comes to stand beside me, I say hello to little Olive. "Hello, sweet girl."

Olive swings out of Sybil's hold and leans right over for me.

"Oh, okay. You want to come to me, a complete stranger." I giggle and coo at her while her little hands grip my shirt, and she even lays her head in the crook of my neck.

"That's something I don't see every day," Delilah says with wide eyes, staring at her daughter. "She usually even hates going to the nanny with Sebastian's girls. That's so weird."

"She must be a good judge of character," Harley says, stepping in beside me.

"This little one is so cute," I gush, getting swooped up in the moment and forgetting that this is the first time I'm meeting this family. After a beat, Olive wants to be put down, so I do, and all eyes go to her. Harley's hand slips into mine, and nerves run up and down my spine. What's his family going to think of him doing that?

I don't pull away, because it's Harley, and I never want to hurt him, and I'm pretty sure we kind of just agreed to a relationship but not in so many words. Neither of us even asked the question.

Mabel, I think her name is, catches my eye and smiles, glancing down at our locked hands. I'm unsure how to react, so I return a grin.

"Come on. I'll take you to talk to Dad," Harley says. We turn to walk, but then Harley whirls around to Delilah. "And we'll be heading over to Dotty's at some stage to work on her mustang."

"What?" Everyone gasps, and shocked looks ripple around the group.

"When did this happen?" Hudson asks.

"It's thanks to Mirella. She asked, and Dotty said yes," he says proudly. This is something massive for them, and they don't even realize the connection they should have with her.

"Good job, Mirella. We've been trying to talk to her for years, and all it's taken is for you to come along. Thank you," Delilah says.

"Anyway, we better go see Dad." Harley practically drags me away.

His siblings are great from that first glance. He did warn me about Tally, and she said hello but didn't really have much else to offer. Aside from that, they were all warm and inviting. I can see myself becoming comfortable around here with all of them. I hope I never outstay my welcome with Dotty because this feels like home. I couldn't leave Harley, Dotty, or the way this area has seeped into my soul. I love it here.

Chapter 18

Harley

WELL, THOSE INTRODUCTIONS WENT BETTER than I could have imagined. The way Olive went right to Mirella was amazing. I had a flash into what my future could be like, and I had to mentally slap myself because there's no way I should be thinking of having a family with her right now. This, us, is something brand new.

"Your family is really nice," Mirella says as we step into the big red barn, heading toward Dad's office. I glance sideways at her. She seems to be taking in the large space filled with workers, horses, vacationers, and clients. It never ends in this place. Always busy.

I lead her into the open door of Dad's office. He sits hunched over paperwork that's spread from one end of his large desk to the other. I can't even see the top of the desk—it's all paper.

"What's going on, Dad?" I'm worried he's taking on too much and will hurt himself in the process. He's only one man, and when he takes it all on, it's not okay, but he hates accepting help. He's like Dotty, in a way.

William growls at whatever's in front of him. "This fundraiser is going to be the death of me. I haven't organized caterers, tents for stalls, workers for rides, or support workers to help with talking to potential clients. I'm not even sure on the theme of this, and that's what is messing me up. All the other years, I've been able to handle it, but this year, it all seems harder." He finally takes a breath and then looks up and drops into his seat. His eyes travel from Mirella to me, then to our hands gripping each other's.

"Well, help has arrived." I gesture to Mirella.

"Hey, I'm happy to help in any way you need. What's the timeframe for when we're supposed to have this fundraiser? It doesn't have to be glamorous and five-stars. Make it so people can come out here and walk around the barn and work pens. Call it a country theme. It's perfect for your ranch," she offers, and it's as if she knows what she's talking about.

Dad eyes her. "It's supposed to happen in the next three weeks. We've done that sort of theme almost every time. I was going for something different this time to try and draw more people."

Mirella nods and gestures to the paperwork. "May I have a look at these? Are they pertaining to the fundraiser?"

Dad nods, and she goes about inserting herself into everything in a good way.

A moment later, she says, "I don't think you should change what you do just to please people. This is your ranch. This is what you do, and you want to showcase that to those who come. You could set up stalls along the cleared spot up your driveway that I can see in the distance. Have a dance floor. Make it fun and inviting. Not so 'black suit and tie.' That's not the vibe I get from you or anyone else here." Wow, she just laid it all out there on Dad.

"You seem to know what you're talking about."

"I studied business economics in college, and I would help my mother prepare her parties, and those ones were formal attire and not your cup of tea. This place? I've been here all of five minutes, and I've seen hard workers and horses who support those who need it. A great family runs it and keeps it going. Why not promote all the good things that exist about this place already?" She shrugs and takes a seat opposite Dad.

Dad says nothing. He's speechless, and I had no idea that Mirella had studied that—or even went to college, for that matter. She surprises me every day. Her confidence when talking with Dad radiates from her. If only I could get her to be that confident on a horse. I'll get there one day with her.

Finally, Dad stands up. "Let's get to work, Mirella. I like your idea of keeping it about us, our family, and what we know. After all, that's what we're about here—family."

"That's wonderful to hear. Let's get to work. It seems like we have lots to do." Mirella's excitement is evident in her voice.

"Okay, I'll leave you two to it. I'll come find you later, Mirella, or the other way around, depending on who finishes first." Leaning over, I kiss her on the cheek and leave. I wish I could be a fly on the wall for what's going to go on in this office this afternoon.

Strong-headed Dad and strong-willed Mirella. This should be interesting.

"Someone's gotten comfortable," Mabel sing-songs as I exit the barn, heading toward the smaller one down the track a little farther. I whirl around. She dances around and stops beside me. "You and Mirella… so it's a thing now?"

"Yeah, I guess so. We kind of spoke about it. We like each other and are comfortable with each other. It's new, so baby steps. She's had it rough with her family and what they want from her, which is how she ended up out here at Dotty's." I start walking again, and she steps in beside me.

"So, she's had it pretty rough?"

"Not in the way you might think, but her family seems to be people who like to push their own agendas on her. From what she's told me, her family is rich. I don't know much else, though. I haven't wanted to probe too much, or I might scare her away."

"Just don't push the public displays of affection on her too much either. She was a little taken aback by you grabbing her hand when you were introducing her to us. She—"

"What?" I ask. "How do you know that?" My tone is accusatory.

Her hands come up defensively. "Whoa, hold on there. I could see it in her eyes. All I'm saying is to just slow it down."

I rub my face with my hands. "Gee, you can tell I don't do this dating thing much. I'll have to talk to her. I don't want her to think I'm pushing anything on her."

Mabel grips my shoulder. "Don't worry about it. I only wanted to let you know," she says softly, and I'm grateful to her for her openness about it.

"Thanks. I'll remember for future reference," I mutter and go on my way to the barn. How could I have been so stupid? And blind.

I work with a majestic horse for most of the afternoon. As I'm packing up, the squeak of the barn door draws my attention. It's Dad.

"Hey, finished up? Where's Mirella?" I shoot a glance over his shoulder, hoping to see her with him.

He tucks his hands into the pockets of his blue jeans and takes in the area. He hasn't been down here in a little while. Delilah and I just use it as we see fit to train our horses. It's out of the way from the hustle and bustle of the rest of the ranch.

"She's with your sisters and Hudson, preparing things for the bonfire. I like her, Harley. She doesn't hold back her opinion, and over the last few hours, we have sorted out most of the details and marketing tactics for the fundraiser." He grins and shakes his head as if thinking of something. "I was put in my place quite a few times. She reminds me of your mother. She was fierce like that."

"Oh, I remember the fights." I laugh, put the halter back in the closet, and turn to face him. "Mom came out on top most of the time, and if she was wrong, she'd be the first to apologize."

"Always." Dad's gaze falls on the horse. "She's a beauty."

"She is. I'm thinking of giving her to Mirella. The horse seems to settle around her and come near her, so I was going to get her to help me with the training. If that's okay with you?" I wouldn't normally ask permission. I'm mostly asking if she can have the horse, because it was Dad's business's money spent to get her.

Dad nods. "I don't mind. I'm sure she'll love it." He shuffles his feet but doesn't elaborate on his comment.

"Is there something on your mind, Dad?"

"There is, actually. Mirella told me about you going to train Dotty's horse with Delilah. Please be respectful. I know we've had our differences, and she can come across quite cranky most of the time. Be respectful," he says gently, as if pondering something else. He opens his mouth and then shuts it.

"We're always nice, Dad. You and Mom told us to be, and we always have been. Nothing is going to change. I'm actually excited to work with the mustang. It's going to be a good challenge. Between Delilah and me, I'm sure we'll work some magic with that beauty," I say and lean up against the wall, waiting to see what Dad is going to say next.

"The challenge will be good for you. Anyway, I do like Mirella, and I appreciate you introducing us and am thankful that she's able to take on everything. I can at least get other things that need to be done, done."

An idea starts to form in my head, and even though the thought of entering that place again makes me uncomfortable, I think this would be perfect for Mirella. "Hey, Dad, I've had an idea. I think it would be good. How would you feel if Mirella moved into Mom's cottage? We could freshen it up and change things that need to be changed. I am fine with you saying no. She doesn't even know that I've asked. Like I said, it just came to me."

Dad rubs his chin while silent. "Let me think about it. That's a special place for all of us. It's also a place that haunts you. Are you going to be okay with going in there to spend time with Mirella?"

I didn't think he'd noticed. I was wrong. "You make a good point, and it's something I'm going to have to work through. Thanks for thinking of me. Let me know when you've decided." I clap him on the shoulder, and we head out, back up to the homestead to help the girls out.

We walk in silence, and my thoughts turn back to the cottage and Mom. It's time to stop holding onto the fear of what I might find when I go in there. This is a new beginning, and it's been such a long time. The pain is still fresh some days. I don't think the pain of losing a parent ever leaves you. It's as though I have a missing spot in my heart, and nothing can fill it. Though, perhaps Mirella could help heal it so it's not a gaping wound anymore.

Chapter 19

Mirella

"DO YOU THINK YOU COULD teach me to ride?" Delilah and I stand away from the group surrounding the raging bonfire. It's too hot to sit near it. The food table is more my style. Harley mingles and chats with guests. It's not that I don't want him teaching me, but I am trying to get to know the members of his family better, and after hearing so much about Delilah being the horse whisperer, I've been drawn to her.

"Don't you want Harley to teach you?"

"I would, but I worry that he'll hover to make sure I don't hurt myself. I'm not great with animals. I'd love for you to teach me if you have time while you're here," I say.

Delilah's face lights up. "I'd love to."

"You tell me when and where, and I'll be there." Excitement ripples through me, but also fear because, hello, big animal that might crush me to death.

Delilah laughs. "Don't look so scared. You're good with me or anyone around here, actually."

"Thanks. I appreciate it."

"How about we start tomorrow?" she offers and waits for my response, which isn't immediate.

The nerves kick into overdrive. I was hoping for a little breathing room, but I don't think that's going to happen now. Finally, I say, "Sure, sounds good. I'll have to come over maybe mid-morning, so I can do my things for Dotty and then get a few more things done with your dad to do with the fundraiser, then I'll be all yours."

"Don't be scared. You'll be a professional after I'm through with you, and that fear you've got will be nothing more than a memory. While you're with Dad tomorrow, Harley and I are going to go see Dotty about her horse. What's the horse like? Last time I saw it, it was pretty wild."

I chuckle. "It still is. Nothing she seems to do is working, or she's not giving it enough time. I don't know. I have no clue about training, or horses in general, or riding. This whole ranch-life experience is brand new to me." I rub my arm nervously, looking out over the group of people hanging out and enjoying each other's company. William and Hudson grill the steaks, and I catch Mabel carrying containers down to an empty table.

"I think it's beginning to suit you more than you realize. From that day I first met you on the wild horse to now, I see great change. Being out here, where there's only nature and peace, is a way to heal in your own time. Trust me. I know all too well the healing process after so much hurt and damage in my life." Her gentle words hit me right in the chest, as if it has a target on it, and she was aiming right for it.

"Harley hasn't really told me much of your story. He's told me a very abbreviated version, and I understand that. We all have our secrets, and that's just the way it goes sometimes." I shrug.

"All I ask is that you try not to hurt Harley," she says. My eyes become wide, and I go to respond, but she stops me. "I'm not saying you're planning to. I see how taken he is with you, and sometimes, he has a tendency to fall in headfirst without thinking of the full story and what consequences might follow. That's Harley. Always has been." She grins, and it touches her eyes. She clearly cares deeply for her brother and family.

"I'm not out to hurt him. At least, it's not my intention to." I try and offer a small comfort. It's not in my nature to cause someone that kind of hurt. I've been hurt, pushed and shoved by my own family, and I never want to do that to someone I care about.

"Oh, I know. I'm just doing the big-sister duties. It wouldn't be right if I didn't since I missed three years of doing it. I'm catching up." She laughs, and the tightness in my chest loosens slightly. Big families can be scary. There are so many people to get on the good side of and please in a way. I do hope they like me and accept me.

The sun disappears, and soon, the stars litter the sky. Laughter surrounds me as I sit around a warm fire with a group of people I've only just met, but it's as though we've been friends forever. Harley's sisters are amazing, but Tally still hasn't warmed to me. I've been told that's normal for her, though. She takes a while to warm up to people. That's cool with me. I'm not going to force my friendship on anyone who doesn't want it. Give her time—that's all I need to do.

"Where are you from, Mirella?" Mabel asks as she takes a bite from her massive burger. I wasn't sure her mouth was going to open wide enough for it, but I was wrong.

I swallow my mouthful of food. "I'm from New York."

A hum of "oh" fills the area.

"What are you doing all the way out here?" a random person asks. She is a guest here, I think.

"Just a change of scenery. It's been so good to get away from it all." I grin around at the faces staring. A slice of uncomfortableness cuts through me as all eyes gaze my way. I'm sure there are more interesting people here than little ol' me.

"It is lovely to get out of the city. We're from New York, and we come here every year at this time just to have a break and live in the silence and nature," an elderly man says, giving his wife a little smile, which she returns. That's what I want. A marriage that lasts all the years, all the arguments, and that still involves looks at each other like that.

The night continues, and the fire soon becomes hot coals. All the guests have gone to bed, as have Delilah, Olive, Tally, William, and Odette. It's just me, Harley, Mabel, and Sybil, laughing at stupid things around the fire.

"Anyway, I better get you home before Dotty has heart failure." Harley rises from the spot beside me, and his warmth is instantly lost. I don't like the coolness.

I get up and take his hand. "Sounds good. I need to get home. Got a busy day tomorrow."

"Yeah, dealing with Dad is a lot for anyone," Harley jokes, and the girls' laughter brings a smile to my face. I backhand Harley in the stomach. He flinches forward.

"Oh, stop it. It can't be that bad. I've already dealt with him, if I remember correctly," I state with raised eyebrows.

Harley squeezes my hand and says, "I'm only kidding, and yes, you were a champion. Not many people can give it to him straight like you did. Pretty much only us, his kids, do that."

The girls nod their agreement, and we say our goodbyes.

Harley leads me to his truck and opens the passenger door for me. "Thanks," I say and climb in. He jumps in and starts the engine, and we're off down the dirt track.

"Did you have fun tonight?" he asks with his eyes straight on the road, the headlights leading the way.

Reaching over, I place my hand on his leg. "Yes, I did. So much fun. Also, I have a riding lesson with Delilah tomorrow."

He takes my hand in his, rubbing his thumb over the back of my hand. It's a small, simple gesture that speaks volumes. "I heard. Delilah told me. I'm glad you asked her."

I sigh with relief. "I just want to get to know members of your family, and you've spoken highly of Delilah, and I want a chance to be taught. Not that you couldn't teach me, but you make me nervous," I say shyly, hoping he's okay with that.

Suddenly, he turns the car in a different direction. "There's something I want to do, and I want you with me while I do it."

"What? Now?" I'm completely confused by this sudden shift in direction. What is going on?

Chapter 20

Harley

THIS ISN'T WHAT I'D PLANNED. I was going to take her home and then go back home, but the way she is talking about wanting to know my family and learning to ride... it confirms for me what I already know. I love this girl, and I don't want to drop her home yet. I want to spend as much time as I can with her.

Mirella glances around to see where we're heading and then back at me. "What are you doing? Aren't you dropping me home?"

I shake my head. "No, I want time with you... alone. If that's okay with you." I glance quickly at her. She doesn't hide her smile.

"I think I'm going to be tired tomorrow." She chuckles, and I know she's right because I'm going to be the exact same way.

We pull up at the cottage. Its silhouette rises in the darkness. We sit a moment until I finally say, "I'm going to need your help."

"What for? It's just the cottage." Her eyes go wide, and all she says is, "Oh."

"Yeah, after not going in there for so long, I think it's time, and I want you with me. I know this is a stupid time of night, but you're here. If you can fight your own demons by going horse riding, then I can face mine, even though they are on different scales. I just want you here."

Mirella leans over and kisses my cheek. "I'm here."

After another moment, I finally climb out, and she follows, my breathing heavy and shaky. I didn't think I'd ever step foot in this cottage again. It needs to happen, though. Mirella is by my side in an instant. "We'll do this together. I'm here for you."

I lead her to the side where the power unit is and flick the switch. The only light to come on is the porch light. We head back around the front, and with a deep breath from me, we take the steps one at a time.

"Do you want me to go in first?" Mirella offers. I nod, and she does.

She heads in and comes back out. "Okay, I've been in, and it's still beautiful inside. I'll be right beside you." She doesn't let go of my hand, and she twists the familiar squeaking doorknob, which is followed by the creak of a door that needs a little oil on it.

A musky scent hits my nose. The place has been closed up for so long, and I'm not sure the girls have been out here much to maintain it. It holds many memories for each of them separately. If we couldn't find Mom at home, she was here, reading or simply sitting and taking in the peace that being out here in the silence could bring.

"I'm not sure where the light switches are in here, and it's pitch black. You might have to do this part," she says. We step into darkness, and right away, my hand goes to the switch beside the door we came through. I flick it on. Brightness fills the room, and I'm swept back into the past, to that day.

I'd walked in here, calling out to Mom. The silence caused me to panic as I ran straight for the bedroom she liked to lie down in. Upon reaching the doorway, I stopped, my heart racing as I rushed to her, then dropped to my knees. Thankfully, she was still breathing, but that memory caused me so much pain and grief. I should have come down to the cottage to see her sooner, and I didn't. What if I hadn't come at all? I almost didn't. It was only because Dad had asked me to check on her that I did. He didn't tell me until much later that she'd had a rough morning already.

I remember being so angry with him. He should have been with her, there to catch her if she fell. He wasn't. I was there to bring her back to the homestead. All the while, I'd never felt as much panic as I did in those moments. I couldn't breathe, talk, or steady my heart. It broke the day I found her, and then we lost her not long after that. I blamed myself. Still do sometimes.

"Are you doing okay?" Mirella's sweet yet concern-filled voice brings me back to the present.

"Yeah," I breathe while soaking up the room's contents. It looks exactly as I left it that dreadful day. "It hasn't changed at all."

Sheets cover the old-style furniture that Mom loved so much. They weren't the comfiest things, but she loved them, and that was what mattered.

Mirella stays close by me, our hands entwined, and I'm so thankful to her for doing this with me. I walk out of the little living area, through the kitchen to the bedroom off to the side. I hover outside the closed door. The fear gripping me becomes tighter.

"Talk me through it. It might help," she offers as we stand there.

"This was the room I found my mother in the day she collapsed." I choke on the words, the emotions of this moment becoming too much. Tears fill my eyes as I recall her limp body sprawled out on the timber floor of the bedroom.

"I'm so sorry, Harley." She hugs my arm to her and gets close. It's her who takes the initiative, and after a moment, she grips the handle, twists it, and pushes the door open. Then, she reaches to the side where the switch is.

When the room lights up, those familiar yellow curtains haunt me, and I want to burn them. I slam my eyes shut.

"Can you tell me about some of the good times coming here to visit your mom? Maybe talking about those times will help overpower the painful memories," she offers, and I feel her step away, the floorboards creaking under her feet as she makes her way into the room. "When you're ready, step inside with me, and I'll be here with open arms, waiting for you."

I finally open my eyes and stare right into hers. Concern radiates from them. "I remember when I got my heart broken by the first girl I apparently loved. She broke up with me for one of my friends—who is no longer my friend, let me just say." I chuckle at the memory of me punching him in the face. It felt good that day.

"Oh, that's horrible."

"It's okay. He got what he deserved. Anyway, Mom told me that the good girls are rare. So rare that they'll show up when you least expect it. She was right. I just had to wait that little bit longer for the black-haired beauty to come riding in on a wild horse. See? Very rare." We both laugh, and Mirella opens her arms for me, waiting.

I step inside and scoop her up in my arms, lifting her off the ground. The lavender scent of her hair soothes me. It's not such a scary place in here with her beside me. Mom wouldn't want this cottage to become a pile of rubble.

"Will you help me clean up at some point? I know we both have a lot on our plates right now with you helping Dad and everything."

"I'd love to help," she says, then kisses me hard, stealing the words I was going to say. She tastes like beer and something sweet. I could kiss her for the rest of my life.

Our kiss deepens, and it's clear she wants more. Her breaths are heavy. She pulls me as close as our bodies can get. It still doesn't seem to be enough. "I can't do this in here," I say between our broken kisses. This room was the one my mother enjoyed, and it's not even the main room of the house.

Scooping her up and out of that bedroom, I head toward another room off the living area. Again, a sheet covers the mattress, and there's a made bed beneath it. I pull it off gently so as not to disturb the dust too much. It's not the most ideal place, but I crave her, and to know that the feeling is returned and that she wants this as well leaves me unwilling to wait.

I lay her down on the mattress of the wooden-framed bed. I stand over Mirella. Her chest moves up and down rapidly. Slowly, I lean over her. Our mouths connect, and sparks fly.

She pulls my shirt up and over my head and throws it to the side. Her soft hands roam my bare chest, each movement causing goosebumps to ripple over my skin. I stare down at her. Her eyes glitter from the moonlight shining in through the window above the bed.

I press my forehead to hers and breathe her in. Without thinking, I say, "I love you, Mirella."

The moment those words leave my mouth, panic sets in. What if she doesn't feel the same?

What if she runs?

Chapter 21

Mirella

I STOP BREATHING AND TRY to process what he just said. He told me he loved me. I'm not sure what to say. I mean, I do have strong feelings for him, and we've come such a long way in a short amount of time. I worry about saying those words and things changing or something. I've never been in a relationship where those three words have been spoken. Not even my parents have said them to me since I was a kid and started back-talking at every possible moment.

"It's okay for you not to say anything. I'm sorry it just came out, but I'm glad I told you, because I want you to know how much I care about you, about us, and what becomes of this relationship." He gently brushes a loose strand of hair from my face.

"I'm speechless. Harley, I have strong feelings for you, and it's not that I don't love you. I know I will. I'm just not ready." Tears fill my eyes as I speak words that would break any man's heart.

Harley presses his lips to mine. "I understand," he says with a gentleness that tells me he truly is different than the other men I've met.

"I do care deeply for you, Harley. Don't doubt that for a moment. If I didn't, I wouldn't be here in this room with you." I trace my fingertips along his tight chest and then his back.

"I know. Don't worry," he breathes. He peppers kisses down my neck and then pulls my shirt up. His gentle hands caress my body in a way it never has been caressed. His tenderness steals my breath, and I'm lost in him and this moment. There's nothing but love and care in here with us as we've both overcome our fears and losses.

After a quick goodbye with Harley this morning, I race home. Our night was spent enjoying and memorizing each other with our lips and tongues. I've never felt so loved. He has a way of making me feel special. I hated racing off this morning after scrambling back into my clothes, but I know Dotty is probably going to be freaking out.

Harley laughed so hard at me. "It's like you're a schoolgirl about to be scolded for staying out. You're an adult, Mirella. Stop stressing."

After seeing the panic in Dotty the day I went missing, I don't ever want to cause her pain again.

She's out back, feeding the chickens. When she spots me, she smiles. Wow, that's not what I expected.

"Sorry! I should have messaged you," I call as I race past to get to the shower and get ready for the day.

"It's okay. Don't stress."

I pause and turn to face her. "Is something wrong? This isn't you." I take a few steps back in her direction.

"No, nothing is wrong. I just know girls your age. I hope you were safe and not into too much mischief."

If only she knew the truth. "No, Harley and I hung out until late at the cottage and lost track of time." The sun is now fully up, and I'm already late to do my chores for Dotty. "I'll be right back down to do what I have to. I just need to have a quick shower."

After my shower, I'm pulling on another pair of jeans when there's a knock at my bedroom door. "Yes?"

The door cracks open, and it's Dotty. She's holding a box in her hands. "These are for you." She hands me the box.

"Oh, Dotty, what for? I don't need anything."

"Hush, you do need these. Go ahead and open it." She watches me intently.

I glance at the box and lift the lid. Inside are a pair of black-and-red boots, fully suitable for all kinds of work around here. And they're no doubt waterproof because, dang, when there's mud, it's horrible. "Oh my goodness, Dotty, these are perfect." I squeal and leap off the bed, placing them down and wrapping her in my arms. "Thank you so much."

"Here," she says. I release her, and she hands me some new thick socks. "You'll need these as well."

"I can't wait to try them on. I really appreciate it." I think back to my conversation with Harley and his comment about my inappropriate footwear. Wait until he sees these.

"It was nothing, dear. It's about time for you to have a pair. Out here, boots are a girl's best friend. You never know what you're going to step on or need to fight off." We both chuckle, and she exits the room, allowing me to finish getting ready, and I can't wait to pull these new babies on my feet.

I break off the packaging from the socks and pull the paper from inside the boots, inspecting them. From the corner of my eye, I spot the journal poking out from under my pillow. "Crap, I'm glad Dotty didn't see this." I pull it out and once again study it, wondering what I should do with it. I flip to another entry, this time skipping ahead a little.

Things are progressing between William and me. My belly is huge. I'm scared of what size this baby is going to be. So long as it's healthy, I'll be happy, but my private parts probably won't be.

Last night, while lying in bed, William was beside me. I want him here now. It's his place. The baby was kicking, and I told him he could touch it if he wanted to. He made sure I was okay with him doing that. I assured him I was.

His warm hand rested on my belly. I took his hand and guided him to where the baby was kicking. I watched his face as it lit up when he felt the kick. It was right then, in that moment, seeing the joy on his face for a child that wasn't his, that I knew I loved William, and I told him so.

I also told him how thankful I was to have him in my life. Since then, our love has been blossoming like a blooming flower in the spring.

More soon,
Olive

I stare down at the page. How fitting for me to read this after what happened last night. I'm so glad Harley didn't force the issue, and we still had an amazing night of growing together as a new couple. I couldn't have asked for anyone better.

I skip a few more entries and go to another one. I don't want to read every single one, but I'm sure Harley and all Olive's kids would want to learn about their parents and how they fell in love. I will give it to Harley.

We had a beautiful baby boy a month ago. I've been so caught up in being a new mom that I haven't been able to journal as much as I once did. He was a big boy, 9lb 7oz, with a head of thick, dark hair and the chubbiest cheeks. That new baby smell is still hanging around, and I love sniffing him. We named him Hudson William Reily.

I am so full of love for these two men. I only wish Dotty would be a part of his life. She came to see him at the hospital and has only visited when Mom has come down, too. We've never been on our own to be able to hash things out. I'm not even sure she wants to anymore. It appears to have become a normal thing for her to not have a relationship with me, her sister, or her nephew. It breaks my heart and also makes me angry.

I'm not going to let myself dwell on it anymore. I am sad to have lost my sister, but I can't keep forcing things. I'm going to love my family and cherish them till the day I die.

More soon,

Olive

Hudson sounds like an adorable baby. I think it's time I give this to Harley, or even William, but will he do what needs to be done?

I flick through, right to the last entry. It's dated a couple of days before Olive passed away. Maybe her last wish was for Hudson to learn the truth.

This could be my last entry. I can't believe this one thick notebook is full of so much of my life. Given the fact that I didn't write daily in my journal, I've still written out the memories my children will have and know about.

I have written each of my children a letter, and hopefully, when they read it, they can forgive me. I've even left one for Dotty, whom I haven't spoken to in many years. I'd love to be able to mend this bridge before I leave this earth, and I know that time is coming. My family isn't aware of how worn out I am. I've let them believe I'm doing okay, which is a lie. I don't want to burden them.

Dotty will know where to find the letters. They are in our special place. She'll know what I mean, so this means whoever finds this will have to go and talk to her. I have desperately wanted to tell Hudson the truth these past few months, but William has talked me out of it so many times. It's not what I want, though. He needs to be told. I'm not going to be here to help him through that big news, and for that, I'm angry with myself. I'm angry at cancer and everything, but one thing I will never regret is loving William and building a large family and a wonderful home for our children's future.

If you, any of my kids, read this, know that I love you. That my heart will always be with you through all that you do in this life. Make it a great life. Fall in love many times. Create a strong family unit. And above all else, love each other through thick and thin.

I love you all.

No more from me,

Olive

Tears stream down my face as I read that line. *No more from me.* She always used to sign off with *more soon.* That was her last entry. My heart breaks that she never got to sort things out with Dotty, and that she never told Hudson because it was what William wanted. It shouldn't have been like that. They should have told him from the very beginning. Now he's a grown man, and he might resent being lied to his entire life.

I could choose to not say anything, but that's not what Olive would have wanted. She wanted to tell Hudson, and so I'll give this to her family. I'll take it over when I visit.

I race to put my new boots on, and they fit perfectly. Dotty must have done some investigating when my shoes were outside covered in mud. I'm so happy. This is the best gift I have ever received. It's meaningful.

I head back downstairs to a travel mug of coffee sitting on the counter. I snatch it up and head out to find Dotty. She's by Black Beauty's round pen. When I get there, I stop. Delilah and

Harley are in there with her, and Dotty is watching from the outside.

"Oh, hey. I thought you guys weren't coming until later?" I ask. I am heading over there soon to do some work with William. He's bringing in people today to shoot some marketing videos and take photos so they can be used for advertising.

"We were, but we wanted a head start. Dad said those people won't be here until after lunch, so when we finish here, you can come back with us," Delilah says as she watches Harley make an attempt with Black Beauty.

He stretches his hand out and slowly moves closer to her. She's a temperamental thing. Her ears are pinned back against her head. I've learned that's a sign of a horse's unhappiness.

"She hasn't been an easy horse to work with," Dotty says to Delilah softly so as not to startle the horse while Harley is working with her.

"Where did you get her from?" Delilah asks, her eyes trained on Black Beauty.

"I bought her from down the road. One of the other ranchers was selling up because the bank was taking the property from them, and the owner asked me if I'd take her. I couldn't let her go to the slaughterhouse, which is where she was going to end up if I didn't."

"Oh, that's horrible for them, losing their house. Who was it?" Delilah said sadly.

"It was the Randal family."

Delilah whips around at the name. "No way. Not the lovely elderly couple?"

Dotty nods. "Yeah, that's them. They couldn't make payments, and none of their kids wanted to help them out. Rude things. I mean, their parents have done so much for them, and that's how they repay them? Too busy off living their lives." Dotty clenches the bar in front of her.

"That's horrible. They'd want to hope I never see their sorry faces again. How many kids did they have?" Delilah asks.

Dotty is silent a beat, then says, "They had four boys I think, and when they came of age, they all just shot off and didn't look back. One, I think joined the army. The other three, I'm not sure about."

Delilah crosses her arms. I'm intrigued by this conversation because, out here, it's a small community. Hearing about someone losing their family home? That's devastating. "What happens to their place now?" I ask.

"It'll most likely get sold," Dotty responds, her mouth downturned.

"Good job, Harley." Delilah grins widely. I glance out to where he is. Black Beauty is close to him. His hand is on her nose, giving her a small pat as he talks gently to her.

"That's really good. With me, she usually runs away," Dotty says.

"Do you mind if we come back every day to work with her? Between Delilah and me, we could have her rideable in no time. Still would be a couple of months," Harley says and makes his way over to us and leans against the fence, still in the pen, leaving Black Beauty alone for a moment.

Dotty shakes her head. "No, come back any time. Even if I'm not home, just come through. I'm sure Mirella will most likely be with this one here." She gestures to Harley, who actually blushes.

"Sounds good. We'll get back home. Things to sort out, and Dad needs to see Mirella." Delilah jerks a thumb at me.

"Oh, hey, nice boots," Harley says excitedly and rushes to inspect them. "Good quality too. Where did you get them?"

I give Dotty a sideways glance. "Dotty got them for me, and I love them. Thank you again."

She waves her hand. "It was no problem at all."

"Now, you're a real country girl with your boots," Harley says, and we all laugh.

I say goodbye to Dotty and tell her I'll message her, and we head over to Rose Ridge Ranch. Harley keeps throwing me playful glances while I sit in the backseat.

"You two couldn't be more obvious," Delilah says, chuckling.

Harley whirls on her. "What are you talking about?"

"You really think I didn't hear you come home in the wee hours of this morning? I bet this one back here was the same. I could have asked Dotty," Delilah teases in a mocking tone.

"Shut up." Harley shoves his sister in the arm.

I love seeing the banter between them. I wish I had siblings I could turn to like these guys do. I'd love a big family, but I may reassess that after I go through childbirth the first time.

Chapter 22

Mirella

Upon arriving at Rose Ridge Ranch, I'm thrown into the deep end, organizing photos and videos. They want videos of training and the staff working with clients, so we need the visitors' permission for that, and we've got Odette and Devon to be on some clips to show and tell what goes on at the ranch. I'm even going to be in a few clips, and that is okay with me—anything to help out. I lead a horse around, and that alone sets off my anxiety.

We've been going for a few hours when it is finally time to call it quits, and right away, I want to go home to bed. I am so tired. Looks like that riding lesson will have to wait for another day.

I yawn and rub my face.

"Good job today, Mirella," William says as he comes and stands next to me.

"We got a lot done." I lift my folder with notes scrawled all over the page. "We have tents and things arriving not next week but the week after. Catering is sorted, and we'll have some food trucks for variety as well. The workers will be on that day to assist with showing people around because you can't be everywhere. Your kids are going to help out, and then there's me, of course." I take a deep breath. "I think we're all sorted and ready to go," I announce.

"I couldn't have done it without your help. I might pull you back in for the next one."

"I don't mind helping." I smile.

Harley comes running over, interrupting my conversation with William, and takes my hand. "Are you free now? I want you to come down to the small barn with me. I'm going to teach you how to train the horses," he says.

"Just be careful because she's new to ranch life, and horses can be scary, especially if she's not spent much time with them before." William's tone is firm, not fatherly.

"I know, Dad. I'll be there. I'm not going to let anything happen to her." Harley pulls me away, and I call goodbye to William, who waves and goes about his business.

The horse is in the round pen off the barn. "Today, all I want you to do is what you saw me doing at Dotty's place this morning. Hold your hand out and slowly move closer. She should eventually come to you. If not, we'll work at it. I'll be just behind you, should you need me."

My hands begin to sweat, and I think my pounding heart is going to burst from my chest or even scare the horse. I do what Harley says with my heart in my mouth, waiting to see what's going to happen.

After a little while and some cooing, the horse comes closer and lets me gently rub her nose. "Harley, look," I whisper excitedly.

"I know. Good job. Now just keep patting her, speak nicely to her, and let her continue to come closer. We'll only be letting her get comfortable with you like this for a little while, and then we will move on to other stuff. She needs to know that you're on her side and that you're not going to harm her. She was treated poorly before she came here. We're giving her a fresh start, and she could possibly be your horse if you can think of a name for her because she desperately needs one."

"I can name her?"

"Yep, just not Princess or anything." He chuckles.

"Oh, now that's a great name," I tease, but deep down, I really like it.

"Just the girl I want to see," Delilah says in a calm voice as she approaches the pen slowly. "You're letting her train?"

"The horse wouldn't warm up to me, but one day, she kept getting closer to Mirella, so I'm trying something different." Harley shrugs.

Delilah nods. "Nice. I do have to let you know that I'm going into town with Mabel and Tally tonight for the next week as we have things to collect for the upcoming fundraiser, and I'm going to pick Sebastian and the girls up from the airport next weekend, so we're making it a sisters' week. So, I'm sorry, Mirella. We'll have to do some riding lessons when I get home."

I tear my gaze away from the horse and smile. "That's okay. You have fun with your sisters. I look forward to meeting your fiancé." I can't help that my grin gets wider. I mean, who doesn't know who Sebastian King is? Formula One superstar. "I'm going to have to compose myself when I do meet him, though." I go back to patting the horse, and she appears to be more comfortable with me.

Delilah, Harley, and I chat for a moment, and then she leaves to go pack for herself and Olive.

"You're doing such an amazing job," Harley says, gesturing to the horse without coming closer. "Look at how much she has warmed up to you. It's almost like she wants to hug you. Let's put her away. All you need to do is grab her halter she's wearing and gently tug her in the direction you want to go."

I do what he asks, and she moves with me. I lead her back into the stall and then exit it and shut the gate behind me, but she comes up and nudges me, demands more attention.

"I'll be back later, girl." With one last pat, I follow Harley and leave.

"Did you want me to walk you home or drive?"

"A walk would be good." I want to talk about last night and what it means. I'm glad he's not treating me any differently. I'd hate for things to be weird between us, because they're really only just getting started, and I don't want our relationship to end.

We set off down the now familiar road, which I've gone down a few times now. I reach out and take Harley's hand. The way he makes me feel with a simple touch is next level, out of this world. My stomach flips and then rights itself.

"How are you after last night?" He beats me to the first question.

My grin gets wider. "It was great. I wouldn't change anything. It was a perfect night, which ended magically." I move closer and press my lips to his cheek. He chuckles and tightens his grip on my hand briefly. "I was going to ask you the same question." The sun begins to hide behind some trees as it descends. I love this time of day out here. The rainbow of colors in the sky lights up my life.

"It did end great, didn't it? I do love you, Mirella, and I'm going to keep saying it unless you tell me you don't want this to go any further. You tell me what you want. I don't want to force anything on you," he assures me. I couldn't have asked for anyone better. He's perfect in every single way. I do love him, but I'm not ready to say it out loud. Doing that really puts things out there, and what if something happens, and we end up fighting, and I leave? Not that I'm planning to, but these things race through my head on occasion.

"Thank you. Like I said, I truly, deeply care for you, and I want nothing between us to change. If anything, I only want our relationship to grow more."

"This time, in three weeks, it's going to be the fundraiser. Won't that be good, to see all your hard work put out there for everyone to see?"

I smile. "I know, it's surreal. I'm glad your dad trusted me enough to allow me to be a part of this."

We arrive at the cottage, and Harley walks me to the fence. "As much as I want to stay and be with you again, I need to get back and have an early night. I feel like I've been a walking zombie most of the day."

I laugh. "I feel the same. A good sleep will do wonders for us both. I'll see you tomorrow," I whisper.

Harley steps closer and takes me in his arms, my hands resting on his chest. In one quick move, his mouth claims mine, and my head is spinning. He kisses with a want and a need. He brings me alive in so many ways. I want to spend every day with him.

He releases me. "I love you, Mirella. I'll see you tomorrow."

With one last kiss, he turns, and I slip through the fence, heading back to Dotty's. I hate leaving him. I love his kindness and comfort. I don't know what my future holds, but I know I want Harley in the picture.

Chapter 23

Mirella

Two and a half weeks later...

"ALL RIGHT, NOW YOU JUST want to walk. Give her a little nudge in the side, and she'll go for you."

I do as Delilah says, and the horse she has me on—Skinny—moves on command. We've spent the last few days getting me used to a new horse because I've become too used to Butter, and Delilah wants to test me out with other horses.

I'm supposed to be versatile and learn to ride different ones. I hate it, but I'm doing it because I want to learn how to handle unexpected situations. Skinny is a good horse. She is friendly enough, though she does have a habit of throwing her head around a little bit. She has a mind of her own. I think Delilah chose her for me for a reason. I needed a more stubborn horse to practice on, especially if I'm ever going to ride the horse down in the small barn, and I really want to because I've been working so hard with her, and we have a great bond forming.

She doesn't like Harley, though, and he can see that. On the odd occasion, she'll let him pat her, but other times, she bites him. It's been quite entertaining. After I finish here, I'll head back down there to do today's training.

"Skinny really has a mind of her own, doesn't she?" I say as I gain more confidence with sitting on her as we ride around the pen.

"She does, and tomorrow, we'll take her out into the fields so we can really test you." Delilah gives me a half grin. "We better finish up here. We have more guests arriving this afternoon who we have to be ready to greet and help get to their cabins. Are you going down to the small barn now? Is Harley waiting for you?"

"Yeah, he is." I tug on the reins, and Skinny stops. I swing my leg over and jump down. I'm so much more confident after having a few lessons with Delilah every couple of days. She's a great teacher. She's even pulled Sebastian and his older daughter, Rylee, out here to have some more lessons with me. Rylee is a natural and shows us all up, but it could be because she's riding Butter, which isn't fair.

"All right, I'll put him away for you. You'd better go do what you need to and get back up here. It's going to be chaos over these next couple of days."

"Okay, I'll see you later." I race off, knowing I'll see her at dinnertime. I've been staying here because sleeping with Harley is so addictive, but I still go back to Dotty's to help out in the mornings. I enjoy spending time with her, and she's been teaching me so many new things. Harley and Delilah have been doing an amazing job with Black Beauty.

I snatch my bag from the bench inside, which contains a water bottle and the journal. I have been trying to find the right time to give the journal to Harley, but I haven't found that moment yet.

As I'm running to the barn, those dark clouds that have been hanging around for days finally start to swell. Rain droplets hit my face. I run faster, and more rain falls. Thankfully, we'd planned for this earlier in the week after checking the weather, and we got the things set up that we needed to. I'm not going to let the rain ruin a good time. So many people have responded and said that they're coming for the event, and a few are staying a couple of nights.

"Phew, got here just in time." I walk in the barn and drop my bag by the closet. Harley is leaning up against the wall, looking at his phone, but the horse isn't out of her pen. "What's going on?"

"I didn't want to pull her out and have it storm. She would freak out, so we'll skip today. I also have something I want to check with you." He grips his hat in his hands, fiddling with the edge.

"Sure. What's that?"

Harley steps closer and takes my hand. He's making me nervous. "So, I know your last name is Jacobson, and a couple checked—"

"Mirella, these people were looking for you," William says from behind me.

I spin on my heel, and my mouth drops to the floor. Amanda and Peter Jacobson, my parents, stand there. My mother's eyes are wide but filled with anger.

"What are you doing here?" I step back beside Harley.

"We've come to take our daughter home so she can get married." My mother tries to sound casual, but there's an edge to her words. It means, *Don't mess with me. You'll do as you're told.*

I stomp my foot. "No, I will not be going with you, and I will not be marrying that jerk of a man. I'm happy here. I won't be leaving. William, please tell them. I'm not leaving." Tears fall down my face, and the people in front of me become blurry images.

"Mirella, it's time to stop this—whatever it is you're doing here," Dad says, gesturing around the barn.

"Mirella has helped us organize the fundraiser this weekend. Why not stick around and see what she's been up to? Harley, could I please have a word with you later?" William asks, his jaw ticking, as is Harley's.

Everything Harley and I have together could be ruined, but I'm not going. I'm not leaving.

"I'm sure she's done a great job, but it's time for her to come home," Mom states. She hasn't changed at all in the months I've been gone. She's joking if she thinks I'm going with them. I won't be going with them. They can't control my life.

"I'm not coming home. Stop saying that. I'm an adult, and you can't make me," I yell.

"Excuse me, don't speak to me like that. We will disinherit you," Mother sneers as if that's going to hurt me.

I laugh. "You're joking, right? I've been out here on my own, without your precious money, and I've made a living for myself. Did you not even hear William? I'm not going with you. That's my final answer." I take off running past Mom, Dad, William, and Harley.

My name is called a number of times as I head down the road toward the cottage, a place where my parents are unlikely to find me. Rain pelts down, drenching every part of me. My clothing is now saturated. I run up the stairs and into the cottage, shutting the door behind me. A split second later, Harley comes in. I run to him. His strong arms capture me as my knees go weak.

We drop to the ground, and he holds me as sobs rip through me, my body shaking uncontrollably. "I've got you," he keeps repeating. Eventually, my body calms, and the tears slow.

"I'm not going with them, Harley. Please know that," I say into his neck as he holds me. I grip his wet shirt.

"I know. I'm not worried. You told me about this, and I'm not angry. I think it is time to clear the air with your parents, whether they listen or they don't." He speaks gently and continues to rub my back, his touch calming.

"You saw how they both were. Do you see a truce happening?"

"No, but state how it is and what you want and then go from there."

"I'm not leaving you, Harley. I love you."

His chest stops moving for a moment.

"Don't stop breathing," I chortle.

"I wasn't expecting it in this moment. You caught me off-guard."

"I couldn't hold back any longer. Plus, the

thought of leaving you—I can't bear it. I love you." I stare up at him. He kisses me softly, and our embrace deepens with each passing moment.

"Come on. Where do you want to go?" Harley asks when we finally break the kiss. "Dotty's or my place?"

"Dotty's please. My parents don't know about her, and at least I won't risk running into them again if I go there." I sniffle, wiping away the wet drips that were coming from my hair.

"Well, our only option is to walk in the rain. Are you okay with that?"

I nod, and he helps me up.

We walk back to Dotty's in silence. I go straight past Dotty on the back porch and into the house. My heart is breaking. Everything was perfect, and now my parents are here, trying to destroy it.

Chapter 24

Harley

I'VE NEVER SEEN HER SO upset. I can't believe her parents are here. I wonder how they found her?

"What's wrong with her?" Dotty asks as Mirella disappears into the house, dripping wet. Mirella's parents being here has not gone down well, and I can see exactly what she means about them being pushy.

"Her parents have shown up, demanding she leave and marry the man they have chosen for her." I sigh, my own heart shattering. I know she doesn't want to go. I hope she stays. I will chase her to the end of the earth if she leaves, and there won't be a wedding of any sort happening unless it's with me.

Dotty's hand flies to her open mouth. "Oh, my goodness. Is she okay?"

I shake my head. "No, she's not. Not at all. Is there anything we can do to help her?"

Dotty rubs her face. "No, this has to be all her. She needs to stand her ground. She won't leave, though. She's happy here. I know it, and you do, too. So, don't worry about it. I'll keep an eye on her for you. I'm sure she'll be over tomorrow, given the fact that it's the fundraiser and that's her baby. She'll be there, but she might need your support."

"Do you think you will be coming?" I ask. She's never come in the past, but she's been good with Delilah and me lately, so I'm hoping she will.

"I will, knowing that Mirella needs my support."

"Thanks, Dotty. Please ring me if you or she needs anything."

We say our goodbyes, and I head back home in the rain. When Dad said he needed to talk to me, I can already imagine what it's about—Mirella and her story.

When I arrive back home, I go straight to his office where he sits. "Dad, what's up?"

Dad peers up over his glasses at me. "Did you know that Mirella was a Jacobson? One of *those* Jacobsons—the rich kind?"

I nod. "Yeah, I did. She has told me things about herself."

"Did she tell you about this marriage?"

"Again, yes. It's not who she wants to marry. It's who her parents want her to marry, which is why she ran away and ended up at Dotty's. She's been hiding out there, pretty much. She hasn't kept anything from me." I straighten my back, defending my girlfriend.

"Okay, I just wanted to check that you weren't getting bombarded by anything you didn't know. She clearly doesn't want to leave."

"No, she doesn't." I sigh. "All I can do is be there for her and wait for her parents to leave with or without her."

"I think it will be without her because she is quite happy here from what I've seen," he offers, and he couldn't be more right.

"She's not going anywhere if I have anything to say about it."

"Good to hear. All right, get back to it. We've still got to run things around here."

I leave the room and go about the rest of my day. Mirella was meant to stay the night again, but I get why she wouldn't want to.

I head up to the house, and it's alive with the others talking about Mirella and her parents. They quiz me the moment I step into the living room.

"She's engaged?" Mabel says in quite a high-pitched voice.

"I knew there was something not quite right about her," Tally says, but I can't deal with her right now.

"Are you okay, bro?" Hudson steps up beside me.

I raise my hands. "Whoa, just stop. She's not engaged. Her parents want her to marry this guy, but she doesn't want to, which is why she ran away and ended up at Dotty's. I'm not explaining it again. She's told me she's not leaving, and I believe and trust her," I announce to them all.

Silence fills the room.

"So, she told you?" Tally questions.

"Yes, she did. Weeks ago. It's not easy for her, having parents like that, so cut her some slack." Turning, I head back out and down to the small barn to feed Mirella's horse and top up her water.

I do what I need to and go to lock up the closet. That's when I notice Mirella's bag and book that must have slipped from it. I collect the bag first and then the book. It drops from my hand, falling open, and some photos slide out.

Crouching down, I notice the handwriting. It's Mom's. Why would Mirella have something with Mom's handwriting in it? I pick up the photos, and they're of Mom and Dad, and there are other people in these photos, too. One almost looks like Dotty.

I flick to one of the entries in the notebook and read it. I drop to the ground, not believing what I'm reading. Dotty is my mom's sister, my aunt, and Hudson isn't Dad's son. My body begins to tremble. Did Mirella just find this and was returning it, or has she had it for a long time? I wonder where she found it. I need to know. But I feel I can't confront her with this today, not with the state she is in. I shove the journal in my jeans and take it back to the house where I put it in my room. My body still trembles after reading those first few entries.

Why were we never told?

Chapter 25

Mirella

IT'S TIME TO FACE MY parents and tell them I'm not going anywhere again. I don't care what they say. I'm not leaving.

Dotty and I drive over to Harley's place. I didn't hear from him last night, which isn't normal for him because he usually messages me goodnight and good morning, but last night and today, I've not heard anything.

All the work I've put in over the last couple of weeks is worth it as we drive into the fundraiser.

Dotty parks and turns to me. "You tell them what you want, and you don't change your answer. Stand your ground. You can stay with me for as long as you need to. I'm not going to kick you out." She reaches over and squeezes my hand. I give her a smile and climb out.

Leaning down, I say, "Thanks, Dotty, for everything."

I shut the door and head to the big red barn where William's office is. He and Harley are in there. Harley's face is stone, unreadable. What's going on with him? Are they fighting again?

"Ah, Mirella, so good to see you this morning. Let's get things going, and hopefully everything falls into place, and the rain stays away just for today." William gets up and walks out. Harley doesn't look at me. Instead, he walks straight past me and out of the barn.

I run after him. "Harley, wait up. What's going on? You do know that I'm not leaving. I've spoken to Dotty, and she's happy to keep me at her place for as long as I need."

He grunts but says nothing. He continues storming away from me toward the small barn. I follow.

When we get there, I stop and wait. I have no idea what's going on. My heart pounds in my chest. Is it about to be broken?

"What is this?" His tone is unkind as he holds up his mother's journal. Crap, I must have left it here yesterday when I ran off.

"Harley, I was planning to give it to you."

"When? I mean, have you already read it?" The pain in his eyes tears me apart inside.

Tears fill my eyes. "I have skimmed through it and caught most of the heavy stuff that I'm guessing you've seen," I answer honestly. "It was always my intention to give it to you."

"How can I trust you?" he yells.

I step back. A fear I've never felt courses through my veins. It tells me to run. This is Harley, though, and he has every right to be angry.

"How long have you had this?" he asks.

"Harley, please, don't be angry. I didn't want to hurt you, and what's in there will surely hurt your entire family. I found it the day you caught me in the cottage for the first time." My voice shakes, and I try to move closer to him. He shifts away and starts pacing.

"Maybe you should just leave with your parents." His cruel words hurt in so many ways.

"I—I told you, I'm not leaving. I love you. Please don't hate me, Harley," I plead my case, but I can already see that I'm losing. I'm going to lose the one man I've ever loved.

"I want you gone!" he roars.

My eyes pop open wide. I'm unable to comprehend how he spoke to me. "I'm not leaving."

Tears drop down his face. I want to wipe them away, but he won't let me near him. "We're done, Mirella. I don't want you here because I can't trust you."

"Screw you, Harley. I was trying to protect you."

He scoffs. "Protect me? You have kept this from me for so long. I can't do this right now with you." He storms past me, his shoulder colliding with mine. I don't know if it was on purpose or not. Dropping to the ground, I don't know what to do but cry.

I rest up against a stall gate and try to calm my unsettled heart. Finally, I get up and step outside, right into the path of Mom and Dad. "Oh great. Just what I need," I mutter.

"Mirella, we aren't trying to be cruel. We just want you home," my mother says.

I get within a foot of her. I tower over her—I take after my dad that way. "I am not going anywhere. I don't care about your threats. I don't care about your money. I want nothing from you, except for you to leave and let me live my life." Gosh, it feels so good to get those words out. I've been hanging onto them for so long.

Turning, I walk away from them and head right to Dotty. "Are you able to take me home? I'm not feeling well. Can you let William know please?"

She nods and races off while I take off to the car where we parked it not long ago.

I need to get out of here. I can't deal with anyone today. Not my parents, nor Harley. I should have known this would blow up in my face.

Chapter 26

Mirella

HE'S NEVER GOING TO TALK to me again. I kept a huge secret from him. My family turned up at the fair because of the publicity the ranch gained. I must have been in one of the advertising videos, unbeknownst to me, and my family saw that and booked a stay at Harley's ranch. Not exactly the reunion I was expecting.

And this morning, Harley decided to look through the journal I'd left in the small barn where the horse is that we've been training. He told me I could name her, but I don't know what yet.

Reading his mother's words must have been painful for him. I'm sure he wants nothing more to do with me. It was never my intention to hurt him or his family. He has a big secret weighing on his shoulders about Hudson not being his dad's son. What is he going to do with that information?

I stand at Black Beauty's pen, and she comes over to me. I stretch out my hand and pat her. She's come a long way since she's been working with Delilah and Harley. I give her a good scratch behind her ear. A couple of months ago, I could never have imagined being this close to horses, but Harley and Delilah have taught me so much with the training we've been doing with his horse and what I've witnessed here.

"What's on your mind?" Dotty steps in beside me. She's become more of a mother figure to me than my own mother, who is currently sleeping over in one of Harley's vacation cabins.

I realize that she doesn't know anything that's gone on or the fact that I know about her and her sister. A knot of nerves tightens in my stomach, and before I can stop them, tears start falling. Her supportive arm comes around me.

"I found a journal that belonged to Olive, your sister." I turn to face her.

Her arm drops, and her mouth slightly hangs open, then she covers it with her hand.

"I'm sorry. I found it a while ago and have been reading it, and I found out about you, her, William, and even Hudson. I wasn't going to say anything because I didn't want to ruin all the good that has been going on around here with Harley and Delilah coming over, to helping them out over there, and then there's Harley's and my relationship, which I now think is over because he found the journal and read it. He got angry at me for keeping it from him, and we haven't spoken since the fair." The words pour, out and tears keep falling. I use the long sleeve of my shirt to wipe away tears and snot. "I didn't want to hurt anyone, and I'm really sorry, Dotty. I understand if you want me to leave."

Black Beauty snickers and huffs. Dotty remains silent. Her hand is still on her mouth, her eyes wide, and she doesn't remove them from me. My heart is broken for all the people involved. Hidden secrets are not healthy. Olive should have told Hudson before she passed and sorted things out with her sister.

"I did reach the last entry in her journal, and she talks about writing letters to each of her family members and putting them in 'the place only Dotty would know.' Maybe it's Olive's way of putting the families together."

Dotty's eyes shimmer with unshed tears. "Where did you find the journal? I knew she kept one but assumed that William had gotten rid of it to keep the family secrets buried."

"It was in the cottage, under the bed, right in the back corner. It was the first time I'd gone out there, and then I found it. I am sorry I didn't tell you." I wring my hands together, hanging my head.

Dotty steps forward and wraps my hands in hers. I glance up into her eyes. "Don't be sad. If anything, I'm glad you found it. I've been angry for so long about something so stupid, and honestly, it's nothing on the grand scale of things. They built a whole new life, and Olive left me out in the cold, and that was probably my own fault because I'd been in love with William for years, and then... well, you know everything. I don't need to explain it to you. It was my own fault, though. Having the kids here working with the horse has been a great opportunity for me to get to know them and learn from them. So, I thank you for that." She pulls me into a hug and kisses my cheek before releasing me.

"What do I do now? Do I try and reach out to Harley or leave things alone and wait for him to come to me?" I need guidance.

Dotty gives me a warm smile. "Come with me. I think it's time we got those letters out and put ghosts to rest so people can start healing."

She takes my hand and leads me up the dirt road I've walked along so many times lately for my meet-ups with Harley and our special times together. I finally got him inside the cottage walls, a place that has haunted him for many years since the passing of his mother. He told me he found her in the bedroom. Could it be that the journal fell from her hands and went under the bed to never be seen again? I hadn't put that together until now.

Dotty's whole demeanor hasn't changed. She is not angry or sad. She's happy and at ease — that would be a better description of her. By the sounds of it, she wants things out in the open and for history not to repeat itself, which was why she was so open with me. "Where are we going?" I ask as we go straight past the cottage.

"Olive and I had a place farther out where we liked to hang as girls. I'm surprised she didn't mention it in her journal."

"No, I don't recall. Can I ask why you never just told Hudson the truth instead of having this pent-up anger, which caused you to be apart from your sister's family for so many years?"

"It wasn't my place to tell, and no matter how much I pushed the matter, William and Olive pushed me away more and more until I just gave up and became the bitter lady you met when you first arrived. You've changed me, Mirella. I wasn't expecting it, but you have, and for that, I'm grateful. You've brought me a peace that I truly needed, and I'm angry at myself for holding onto things for so long." She clears her throat, and we keep walking.

Finally, we come to the edge of the bush I was in when I had my afternoon nap and went missing for the day.

Dotty stops and looks both ways along the tree line. "Uh, this way. It's been so long I had to think for a moment." We veer to the left, and then she starts counting the trees and finally stops at one that has some carving in the wood. Stepping closer, I look at it, and it's an O and D carved into the trunk.

Dotty drops to her knees and starts digging away at the ground. She grabs a stick and loosens the hard dirt until I hear a twang. The stick has hit something metal.

"Here it is," she gasps and finishes digging it out. I help pull away some dirt, revealing an old tin box with Dotty's and Olive's names engraved on it. It isn't neat—schoolgirls did this. It's a memorabilia box.

She pulls it from the earth and goes about unhooking the latches. As she lifts the lid, a sob comes from her lips. "Oh, Olive."

Inside the box, right on top, is an envelope with Dotty's name written neatly on it. With trembling hands, she reaches in and pulls it out. Underneath, there's another with the name Hudson on it.

"Do you mind if I have a look?" I ask gently, not wanting to overstep.

She shakes her head. Tears are streaming down her pink cheeks. She opens the envelope. I pick up the bunch that are inside the tin and read all the names.

Hudson.

William.

Delilah.

Harley.

Mabel.

Sybil.

Talulla.

Odette.

It's a list of apologies, I'm guessing. Their parents kept something so big to themselves, and now it's come to light because of my stupidity. I wonder what would have happened if Olive had gotten the journal back before she passed away. Would she have given it to Hudson or William?

Slowly, I place the envelopes back in the box and wait patiently for Dotty to read her multi-page letter on small sheets of yellowing paper. I've never seen her so torn up and upset like this.

When she finishes, she glances up at me. Tears stain her face, but she's grinning.

"She forgave me years ago. She was going to come and give me the journal to make sure that Hudson eventually knew the truth. She hoped that I'd be there for the kids and William. I have wasted so many years… so many."

Shuffling closer, I pull her in for a hug. "Now it's time we do what Olive wanted," I say softly while filled with worry about what's to come.

Chapter 27

Harley

I CLOSE THE JOURNAL AND place it down beside me on my bed, my hand resting on it. I haven't slept or eaten in the last twenty-four hours since finding this in the barn. I've felt so much anger and hurt toward my father for keeping this from all of us, but mostly from Hudson. He's my brother, no matter what any book says. This is going to break him apart.

After rising from my bed, I head downstairs and into the kitchen where the rest of the family, even Dad, is hyped up and discussing the success of the fair yesterday.

"Harley, Mirella did an amazing job at pulling everything together, especially given the downpour we had." Hudson cheers as I enter the kitchen. "Where is she? Did she stay at Dotty's last night because her parents are in the cabins?" He glances behind me.

"No, she didn't. We got into a bit of a fight over this." I hold up the journal, and cutlery clatters to a plate, and I turn my gaze to Dad to find him staring as though he's seen a ghost.

"What is it?" The question comes from everyone in the open kitchen area.

I know I'm opening a can of worms that will hurt this family — and on such a good day. I can't keep this in, though.

Before I can continue, there's a knock at the door. Mabel rushes off to answer it.

"Harley, what is it?" Sybil pushes again.

"How about, before you start that, you have the rest of what you need?" Mirella announces as she comes into the room with Dotty by her side. She must have told her. Dotty's blotchy face and fresh tears are evidence.

"What's going on here?" William asks loudly, causing an uncomfortable silence.

It's Mirella who starts. "A while back, I was in the cottage along the fence line. This was before I knew any of you, and I was curious. Once in there, I came across this journal under the bed in the same bedroom that Harley found your mother on that awful day." She pauses and takes a breath. "I found that journal Harley is holding and discovered that it actually belonged to your mother, Olive. Upon reading it, I've learned things about your parents, you guys, and even Dotty. I don't think it's my place to say anything more, so I'll let Dotty tell you." Mirella takes a step back, and Dotty doesn't move.

Dotty exhales, then says, "I am your mother's sister."

Everyone around us gasps.

I glance over at Dad, who has become red-faced. "Just when things are becoming good between us, you have to dredge all of this history up. Sometimes things need to remain where they are because people could get hurt," Dad growls at Dotty, who doesn't even flinch.

"I'm sorry you feel that way, William. This is what Olive wanted."

"Oh, how would you know what she wanted? You had nothing to do with her for years. Even when the children were born, you still didn't come," he retorts.

"That's because I didn't feel welcome by you or her. She left me a letter, and in it, she stated what she wanted." Dotty holds up an open envelope.

"And your mother left one for each of you. They were in a place that only her and Dotty knew about. I discovered it in the last journal entry," Mirella says and holds up a bunch of yellowed envelopes. I catch Dad's name on the one in the front.

"Well, let's have them." Hudson rushes forward, but Mirella holds them back.

"There's something you need to know before you read these letters. Each one is personal to the person. William, do you have something you'd like to tell Hudson, or would you like Dotty, myself, or even Harley to, because I'm sure he's read the journal by now," Mirella says and gives me a sideways glance, her hurt evident in her short stare. The words I spoke to her last night are ones I'm not sure I can ever forgive myself for, even if she forgives me.

Hudson turns between us. "Well, who's going to tell me what I need to know so I can read Mom's letter?"

William sighs. "Take a seat, Hud. Actually, all of you should. Even you two, Dotty and Mirella."

Everyone finds a spot at the large dining table. I take in my family, Seb included, and this moment right now is one that is going to stick with all of us for such a long time. I don't think anyone will feel any differently toward Hudson, but this will still be heartbreaking for him. My heart thunders away in my chest.

Tally stares at me from across the table. Questions fill her eyes. Hudson takes a seat beside Dad, and the room becomes eerily silent until Dad breaks it. "Hudson and all of you, I want you to know that your mother and I love you all equally. I never wanted to say anything because I didn't want to hurt anyone."

"Dad, you're kind of scaring all of us," Mabel says, her voice shaking, her fingers wrung together tightly. Tally reaches over and places her hand on hers.

Olive coos, and Delilah hands her some more banana to keep her happy. Sebastian stands. "I'll take her for a little walk. This seems to be a family matter." He takes Olive, Rylee, and Ruby out the back door and to the swing set he's recently purchased for the girls. He's a good man. I'm so glad Delilah found him.

Is this going to destroy my family?

"I'm sorry," Dad says and starts again. "Okay, Hudson, there was a time, many years ago, when your mother was in love with another man. This was before me. And before any of you get the wrong idea about your mom, she had a one-night stand with a man who only thought of himself. I tried to warn her many times, tell her what he was like. He was working on our ranch. My dad was his boss. I guess you could say this was where my anger came out with regards to you and Eli." He turns to Delilah who sits at the end of the table, her chin beginning to quiver as she no doubt fights back tears. She nods.

"Anyway, from that night, she got pregnant. She told the guy, and he left with no word. Just packed his bag and left. Your mother was beside herself." Dad pauses to clear his throat.

"She was very upset," Dotty continues the story. "She came to me and told me about it, and later, one night, she mentioned it to William. Without hesitation, your dad offered to marry her and claim the child as his."

A round of gasps and sobs fills the room.

"So, you're telling me that I'm not your son?" Hudson asks, his face turning a shade of red, and I'm not even sure he's breathing. His chest is moving but a little too fast.

"You're not my biological child, but you are still my son, Hudson. I love you as equally as I do the rest of our kids. You are my son. Don't ever forget that," Dad pleads, a look of anguish plastered on his face, tears in his eyes.

Hudson rises from his seat with such a force that it pushes his chair backward, and it topples over.

"Before you rush off, I have something that your mother wanted you to have." Mirella stands and hands Hudson one of the sealed envelopes, his name written on it, and then she proceeds to hand out the rest to everyone else. Even Odette has one, so she'll need some help with hers. The girls remain speechless while envelopes are torn open and silently read.

I'm not sure I want to read mine just yet. Anger and annoyance at my mom and dad course through me. I hate having these kinds of emotions and having to deal with them.

"I'll get out of your way," Mirella offers and heads down the hallway toward the front door.

A part of me screams at myself to go after her, and the other part is like, *She kept this from you. Let go of what we had.* I can't, though. What kind of relationship will we have if this is something we can't fix? I don't want to lose her. She is everything to me, and I don't want to have a family with anyone else in my life.

Jumping up from my spot, I race back up to my room. In my closet, tucked away on the top shelf in a shoebox, is a ring my mother gave me before she passed. She told me to give it to the girl I was going to marry.

Mirella is that girl. My future.

Chapter 28

Mirella

Turmoil wreaks havoc on my body. The stress of the entire situation has caused me to forget to actually eat. Stepping down from the homestead's front porch step, I wobble. Taking a few more steps, I come face to face with the two people I didn't want to ever see again. Mom and Dad.

Mom's hair is perfectly pinned, and Dad looks mighty uncomfortable out of a suit. Why are they coming up to the homestead?

"Uh, what do you two want? I thought I made myself pretty clear that I'm not going back with you, and I definitely won't be marrying that playboy who can't keep it in his pants," I grit out the last part through my teeth. "And why are you even coming up to the homestead? It's off-limits to the guests."

Mother folds her arms over her chest and gives me her pinched-lip expression. Today, her lips are a shade of pink. "Stop being so rude, Mirella. You should really come home with us and discuss this situation."

I open my mouth to retort when the porch screen bursts open. Harley stands there, his chest rising and falling as though he's just run a marathon.

"She's not going anywhere because I'm going to marry her," he announces, and my jaw hits the ground, as does my mother's.

"Excuse me, I don't think so." She stabs a finger at Harley. Dad simply stands there, saying nothing, and takes in Harley in his cowboy hat, jeans, and an open flannelette over his tee. He's all country, no city, and he doesn't come from bucketloads of money like my family.

Harley laughs. "I really don't think that's up to you, is it? You do realize that you can't always control her. She is old enough to make her own decisions, and she has a job out here working on two properties—ours and the one where she's currently living. You have no say in her life. You may be her parents, but what she wants to do with her life is totally up to her."

Oh, he makes my heart swoon with each word he says. And here I thought he was done with me after keeping the journal a secret.

My mother straightens her back, and my father simply watches the exchange. He's not his usual self. He would back Mom up any other time, but today, he's remaining silent.

"She is already marrying someone, and it isn't you, young man. You can't offer her what someone else can." Mom looks down her nose at Harley, and he doesn't seem fazed by it.

"Have you even asked your daughter, once, ever in her life, what she wants?" He holds up one finger to my mother.

She takes a step back and twists her head to look at Dad. "Aren't you going to interject here?" She slaps his arm. Still, he doesn't move, but he does smile. It's not a fake one either. He's quite good at those.

He steps forward, a foot away from me. "What do you want, Mirella?" Dad asks, his voice soft.

I open my mouth, and then pause, and open it again. "I want to stay here. I don't want to go back to New York. I've created a new life here, and would you believe I actually get to use my college degree?" I beam brightly at my father, whose grin widens.

Without warning, he pulls me in and holds me against him for a moment, then releases me. "You can stay, and if this young man makes you happy, then I am happy."

"Oh, thank you so much, Dad." I squeal and leap at him for another hug, which he happily returns. Tears burn my eyes.

"Wait, no," my mother chimes in with her disapproval, but I don't care anymore. She can hate me and even not come to my future wedding.

Dad releases me and gazes at Mom. "I think it's time we let her make her own choices, or we will lose her forever." Turning back to me, he continues. "When you left and we couldn't find you, I was beside myself," he chokes on his emotions before clearing his throat and says, "I couldn't see what we had done as wrong, but when I came here and saw how much you had changed as a person, it became clear. I want nothing more than for you to be happy. I'm sure your mother will come around eventually. Maybe let her help out with the wedding, and it'll make her happy."

Mom huffs. "Whatever. It's not what I had planned out for her."

"Sometimes broken plans are the best kind," Harley offers. "I love your daughter, even though she might be a little annoyed at me for a few things that have happened as of late. I love her and will defend her from anyone who causes her unhappiness or hurt. She's mine to protect and care for now." He moves beside me and wraps his arm securely around my waist, and I melt against him. We share one love, one heart, and a whole lot of happiness for our future. I couldn't be happier.

"I'm not happy about any of this." Mom waves her hand between Harley and me. "You're my only daughter, Mirella, and I wanted the very best for you. This isn't what I had in mind." Tears fill her eyes, and I know she's softening to the idea of it all. She's not happy, but she'll get there eventually.

I move forward and take her hand. We've never really been the huggy, touchy type of duo who get along. I say, "I know, Mom, but could it be possible for you to give me the benefit of the doubt here? I am so happy. Harley makes me happy. Being here with his family, and even the animals, brings me joy I've never experienced before. I've learned so much about myself and what I'm capable of, especially without the help of my parents. So, if anything, you both drove me to be more determined than ever to prove I could do things on my own. Heck, I even ride horses now and have been helping train one, which will eventually be my own."

Dad wraps an arm around Mom. "Honey, we are proud of you. I wish we had listened to you more and maybe figured things out sooner. If we had, perhaps you wouldn't have run away."

"Hey, I'm all for the running away. I'll be forever thankful for that. Sorry, I know it caused you both pain and stress, but it also brought her to me," Harley offers with a small bow of his head to my parents.

I pull Mom in for a hug, which she amazingly returns, even though it feels awkward. I love her and Dad, and I'm so filled with joy that they have been able to release me in a way.

"I've been thinking," Dad starts and is cut off when Dotty and William come out the front door, appearing quite sullen and forlorn. "Ah, just the man I wanted to see," Dad says brightly, not reading their moods at all.

"What can I do for you?" William says and comes down the steps and shakes my dad's hand.

"My wife and I would like to offer an amount to help with things around here. After walking around yesterday and getting a great view of what you do here for all the clients and vacationers, we wanted to put something toward this wonderful cause."

"Thank you so much. We greatly appreciate that," William says and shakes Dad's hand again. "I'll have some paperwork for you to fill out later if you want. How long are you staying?"

Dad looks adoringly at Mom. "Another couple of days, I think. We have some catching up to do with our daughter, since it's been quite a few months since we've seen her."

"Mom, Dad, this is Dotty. I've been staying at her ranch, which is a neighboring one to Rose Ridge." Dotty's grin widens as I stop beside her.

Dad nods, and Mom does her attempt at a smile of gratitude. "Thank you for taking care of our daughter. We'd like to offer you payment for your help with Mirella."

Dotty waves her hand, dismissing their offer. "No, I don't want it. She's been working plenty to help cover her costs, and it's no bother to me. I was happy to do it." She pats me on the back and then walks past the group and back to her car. Before climbing in, she calls, "I'll see you when you get home, Mirella."

I wave, as does Harley.

He whispers in my ear, "Not before I've had a moment with you to myself."

My cheeks warm at the thought of alone time with him.

"Well, if you'd like to come with me, we can get started on the paperwork. We greatly appreciate your contribution to our ranch and the things we do here." William walks off, and Mom and Dad follow, their chatting becoming more like a mumble the more distance they put between us.

"Harley, I need to sit down and maybe eat something, or I'm going to pass out." All the adrenaline from the moment with Mom and Dad is slowly leaving my body and reminding me that I haven't eaten.

"What are you doing to yourself to get this way?" He hooks his arm around me and leads me upstairs.

"I've not been eating because of the stress of the last twenty-four hours. I didn't know if I'd lost you or not." As I turn toward him, he stares at me, a pained expression on his face.

He leans forward, his mouth claims mine, and I soak up each and every movement and touch, wanting more, wanting to experience what we did the other night together. Each kiss is like a new rainbow of fireworks. The colors explode and bring a new happiness into my life.

He breaks off the moment and sighs. "Plenty of time for this later, but we need to get some food for both of us. Come on. Food is ready up here." He grips my hands and tugs me in the direction of the house.

I dig my heels in. "Won't they all be angry with me for keeping this secret about their mother? Shouldn't you be with your family right now? Didn't you read your letter from your mom?" I fire the questions off rapidly, a lasso tightening around my chest at the thought of his whole family hating me because of this. He might be easy to forgive, but others in his family might not be. Tally, for one. I'm already not sure if she likes me or not. It's been hard to get a read on her.

Harley squeezes my hand, attempting to give me some assurance, but the situation is still not sitting right in my stomach. "Don't worry. I've got you. Whatever you face, I face with you. We do it all together now. You and me."

Chapter 29

Harley

I AM NEVER LETTING HER go. If she is going to be a part of this family in the future, then we'll face the hard things together.

We step back into the house, and there are a few rumblings from the kitchen and living area.

"Let's get you some food," I say softly, not wanting her to pass out because it's my fault she's in this state. That's something we're going to have to talk about later.

We enter the kitchen, and my family falls silent. All eyes turn on us.

"Why didn't you tell us?" Tally barks from the end of the table as she stares daggers at Mirella.

"Tally, we have to recognize the situation Mirella was in when she discovered that secret.

It wasn't her place to say anything. It was Dad or Dotty who should have said something." I head into the kitchen and grab two plates out, not wanting this line of attack toward Mirella to continue.

Mabel walks over and pulls Mirella into a hug. "I know that would have been hard for you. I'm sad that people, especially Hudson, have been hurt because of Mom and Dad's secret. Not that I look at Hudson any differently now."

"None of us do," Sybil replies from the table.

It's when I look up that I notice Delilah and Hudson aren't there. "Where are Hudson and Delilah?"

Mabel tilts her head to gesture to the back door. When I glance out, I spot Delilah and Hudson sitting on the step, talking. Her arm is wrapped around his shoulders, which shake slightly.

"Grab some food," I say to Mirella. "I'll be back." I need to be there for my brother.

I step onto the back patio and shut the door behind me. "Hud? How are you doing?"

Delilah gives me a shake of the head, her mouth turned down and tears in her eyes. She has a wet face. "It's a bit much to take in," Delilah offers softly.

I take a seat on the opposite side of Hudson. I tug the journal out from the back of my jeans. "Here, you probably need to read this to get the full picture of things. I only read it last night and was coming to tell everyone this morning."

Hudson picks his head up from his hands and stares at the book. It's then I notice the envelope clutched in his hand, the top ripped open. "Thanks, Harley. I don't know how to process all of this. What should I do?" He glances between Delilah and me.

"That's totally up to you. We can't give you that answer," Delilah says and rubs her hand over the middle of his back.

"What do you want to do?" I ask.

Hudson shakes his head and scrunches the letter in his hand tighter. "I want to be angry at her and Dad for not telling me the truth. It's not like I was a little boy when she died. No, I was a man, and I should have been told by my mother. I feel so confused and... urgh," he cries out, and my heart breaks for him and what he must be feeling.

"Oh, Hud, I wish there was something I could do to help ease what you're going through," Delilah says.

Hudson gets up suddenly, causing us both to sit back. "I need some time alone. Thanks, guys. Can you let Mirella know I'm not angry with her? I'd hate for her to think this was her fault when it wasn't. I just want to be on my own."

"Not a problem. We'll be here when you're ready," I say and get up, as does Delilah. We watch Hudson disappear around the side of the house.

Sebastian gives Delilah a hug. The girls play happily around the playground.

"Do you think he'll be okay?" I ask Delilah.

She shrugs and shakes her head. "No, not today, or for a little while. He needs to figure this out himself. We can't tell him what to do. Have you read your letter from Mom?"

I shake my head. "No, I was too busy trying to be the hero and get Mirella back. I basically proposed to her in the process, but I haven't given her the ring yet."

"Excuse me? What ring? Proposal?" Delilah's eyes bug out of her head, and her voice rises up a notch.

"Whoa, I haven't told anyone, and I want to do it properly." I reach into my pocket and pull out Mom's ring. It's a simple medium-size white diamond on a golden band with two dark-blue sapphires on either side.

Delilah reaches for it. "Oh, my goodness, that's where this went. To you?"

"Yeah, Mom gave it to me a couple of months before she passed away."

"Us girls fought over this ring once, but I'm glad you have it. And yes, I have read Mom's letter."

"What does it say, if you don't mind me asking?" I'm fine with her not telling me, but curiosity has gotten the better of me.

Reaching into her back pocket, she pulls her letter out and hands it to me. "Here, I don't mind. I think it was intended to be given to us after she'd passed, but I guess the journal got lost and so did the letters along with it."

"Oh, I don't want to be that invasive. Was just after a simplified version." I push her hand back toward her body.

"Here, I don't mind at all. Sebastian and I are going for a walk. We'll be back later," she says, and they both head off in the direction of the playground and grab Ruby and Olive, one on each of their hips. Rylee bounces around their legs, full of energy.

I pull out the piece of paper and read it.

Dearest Delilah,

My biggest girl. I know you're going to be a force to be reckoned with, and you'll most likely give your father the hardest time. I hope that, when you read this, you'll remember that he's only human, and we all make mistakes.

If you're reading this, then I know you know about Hudson and the story there. Your father loves him, and he doesn't care that he's not his blood. Sometimes love is thicker than blood, and that's your father with Hudson.

Dad helped me out in one of the toughest times in my life. He became my anchor and the love of my life, even if I was unsure at the beginning of our marriage. We learned and built a friendship first, and the rest came after. I wouldn't change a thing. Please be there for Hudson. He's going to need his family.

I love you so much, and my only wish is that I could be there when you get married to the man of your dreams. You have such a wild heart, and I know you'll have your challenges, but I'm always here with you in spirit, watching over you.

Forever yours,

Mom

Short, sweet, and to the point. She has hit the nail on the head about Delilah.

I miss Mom. I miss the joy and happiness she brought to our home. When baby Olive and Sebastian's girls became a part of our lives, things around here came alive again. Now, a storm cloud is hanging over us, but somehow, we have to get through this. Together.

Chapter 30

Mirella

THE TENSION IN THE ROOM is thick, almost suffocating. I put some bacon, eggs, and toast on my plate and take a seat. I've never felt more uncomfortable and out of place than I do right now. Mabel is lovely. Odette, with her sweet spirit, is none the wiser. Tally has made her stance clear, but Sybil has remained quiet.

Clearing my throat, I say, "I want you all to know that I wasn't intentionally keeping anything from you. I had planned to tell Harley and confront Dotty about the journal. I wasn't going to keep the secret, but I also couldn't share what I knew because it's not my secret to tell. I do hope you all can forgive me."

"Hudson knows that," Harley says as he comes back inside. "He just told me."

Sybil rises from her spot at the table. "Is he okay?"

Harley comes and sits beside me. "He is confused and angry, which is understandable. He just wants some space right now."

I shovel some food into my mouth so I don't have to speak. This is their family, and it has to heal.

"I'll check on him later," Mabel offers and leaves the room with envelope in hand. Tally and Sybil have theirs ripped open in front of them. I can't help wondering what Olive has written to each of them. She'd have to know the impact of this secret and put something in each of their letters about it.

The talking stops, and there's only the clattering of cutlery and the sound of the faucet running at the sink. I finish my meal, and Harley takes my plate, along with his, to the sink and rinses them off. "Come on, Mirella," he says and waits for me to get to his side.

"Where are we going?" I ask as we leave through the front door.

"To the cottage for a little peace and quiet. It's been a big morning. We can go visit your parents instead if you want?"

"No, I'm okay to see them later."

"Do you want to walk, ride, or drive?" he asks.

The thought of riding brings me a sense of freedom. I didn't feel that in the beginning. It's taken some getting used to, but I'm enjoying learning and stepping out of my comfort zone. "Can we ride?" I ask, hopeful.

Harley doesn't hide his smile. "Yes, we can."

We make our way to the big red barn and check the stalls. Chester and Butter are available to use, so we saddle them up. Harley still checks over all my equipment to make sure I've fastened it all right and that I'm safe.

Harley climbs up on Chester, and then I hoist myself onto Butter, and we walk out of the barn. Glancing to my right, I spot Mom and Dad standing at William's door. Mom's mouth is hanging open, and Dad is beaming. I wave, and we're out the door. I give Butter a little nudge, and she catches up to Chester, and we walk side by side, even though Chester is a little bit taller. It doesn't faze him.

"I'm guessing you aren't angry with me anymore?" I ask as the horses walk down the dirt road, their hooves clicking on the stones.

"I wanted to be," he admits, and my stomach clenches. "I'm not so much anymore because I realize the position you were in. It wasn't your place to say anything. I wish you had told me sooner—actually told me, and not by accidently leaving the journal in the little barn."

I rub my face with one hand. The scent of leather from the reins hits my nose. "I know, and I'm really sorry about that. I had planned to give it to you. I was being nosy and wanted to read it and, I guess, learn about your family. Your mom was a beautiful person, and she only wanted what was best for her children, and perhaps keeping the secret for as long as she did was her way of protecting Hudson. If she hadn't collapsed that day you found her, this all would have come to light sooner."

"That's true," Harley seems to ponder this. "I am so sorry for how I spoke to you yesterday." He looks over at me, and the anguish is in his eyes. The pain.

"I probably deserved it."

"No, no one, especially you, should ever be spoken to like that. I will never raise my voice to you in anger again. I am ashamed of my behavior." He reaches out his hand, and I take it. We ride like this for a moment before he lets go, and we ride the rest of the way in silence.

When we finally arrive at the cottage, there's something different about it. Almost like a cloud over the space has been shifted, and the sun can shine brightly over it once again. Like I imagine it would have when Olive filled the space.

Harley jumps down and then comes to assist me, even though I don't need help anymore. I've finally mastered the dismount, with Delilah's assistance. She really knows her stuff when it comes to horses. She's a true horse whisperer.

"Now, I'd been speaking to Dad before all of this happened. He wants to offer the cottage to you as a place of your own to live. It's close to Dotty's and close to Rose Ridge. Hudson and I are going to put a gate in here." He points to a section of the fence. "I've spoken to Dad and Dotty, and they're both happy about the arrangement. Of course, we might need to do a massive cleanup inside, but I'm sure you won't mind doing that at all."

"Are you serious?" I almost yell. My high-pitched response almost echoes in the hills around us. "Are you okay with that? Given it was your mother's space?"

"Trust me, she would want it being used. Just like the library back at the house. Mom has her special spots all over this ranch."

I launch myself at Harley, who catches me in his open arms. His embrace is warm, wanting, and above all else, loving. "Thank you so much," I say.

He places me down. His hand slides behind my neck, pulling my mouth to his. My breath hitches as every part of me craves his touch. One of his hands slides under my top and pulls me tighter against him. I melt against him, my body throbbing with need.

"I love you so much," he whispers between wet kisses.

"I love you, too." I pull back and say, "I think there's something we probably need to discuss."

His eyes light up. Reaching into his pocket, he drops to one knee and presents me with a beautiful diamond-and-sapphire ring. My hands fly to my agape mouth. "Oh, my goodness."

"Is this what you mean? Mirella Jacobson, from the day I met you on the runaway horse, from the moment you trespassed on our property, till this moment right now, I knew you were the girl for me. The one I wanted to spend the rest of my life with. I love you and want you to be my wife. Will you marry me?"

I take him in briefly. A bead of sweat has formed on his head. The glistening in his eyes holds my gaze. I could never say no to him. I love him, heart and soul. "Yes," I say breathlessly. Harley slips the ring on my finger. It actually fits perfectly. Then, he claims my mouth again. Only, this time, I want more. "Take me inside. I need you."

Chapter 31

Harley

AFTER MY SPONTANEOUS PROPOSAL, I make love ever so slowly to Mirella at the cottage. Thankfully, she took the time a couple of weeks back to at least clean up the bedroom, and now, I've left her to make plans for the little two-bedroom home that will most likely become *our* place since I'm not about to leave her any more.

I had no intention of proposing this morning at all.

I make my way back to the ranch. I need to tell my family, but I'm not sure if this is the most appropriate timing, given everything that has come to light today.

After putting Chester back in the barn and unsaddling him, I take off down to the small barn to work with Mirella's horse that she still needs to name. Stepping inside, I spot Hudson on the floor, in the dirt, leaning against the wall.

"Hey, man. You doing okay?" I head over to him and drop down beside him. This isn't my fun-loving brother. Here before me is a shadow of the man he was before he found out that Dad isn't really his dad.

"I've been better. I don't know what to do, Harley. Do I do anything? Should I even bother to look for a man who didn't want me?" His voice cracks. The world that he knew has been shattered.

"I can't tell you what to do, but I can offer some advice. If you don't want to go look for your biological father, then that's okay. On the birth certificate, Dad's name is listed. He's been there for everything. He is your father. The other man is just a donor. Did Mom have much to say in her letter?"

He shakes his head and drops his face into his hands. "She told me his name. She also told me that she had looked him up and that he has a family of his own now. His son is actually rich. I've searched them. The man who left Mom... his name is Ryan Andrews. I mean, I have a whole other family out there I know nothing about. Would you want to know them?" His pleading eyes come up and meet mine.

Wishing I could give him the answer he wants to hear, I shrug. "I can't say what I'd do in your position. If you feel a desire to know them, then do it. You have every right to meet them. Perhaps, after all this time, Ryan might hold some guilt over what he did."

Hudson clenches his fist, and his jaw ticks. "I would never leave a pregnant woman. Can you punch me if I ever have the thought? Even if the mother and I don't stay together, I want to be a part of my child's life. I would never do what he did."

Resting my hand on his shoulder, I say, "No, you wouldn't, because you've been raised right by parents who love you."

"I'm sorry about all of this. I feel like this mess is on me, when I know it really isn't, but still."

"You have nothing to apologize for. This has turned things in our family upside down. I mean, we have an aunt we've been fighting with since we were little and, well, all your news. It's kind of shaken things up a little, but I'm sure it's nothing we can't get through together. I've got you. So does everyone else."

"Thanks, Harley."

"I do have something I want to tell you, though."

"Sure. What's that?"

"I asked Mirella to marry me, and she said yes."

Hudson's face lights up, and it's the happiest I've seen him all day. "Bro, I'm so excited for you. You have brought me news that I needed to hear today. I'm so happy for you both. Bring on two weddings! We need a good party around here." It's his turn to clap me on the back. He seems like his usual self.

"Want to come with me to tell the rest of the family? Because some of the girls aren't on Mirella's side."

Hudson's brow furrows. "Why? It's not like she's done anything wrong."

"I know, but try telling Tally that. She's always out for a fight, that girl, and doesn't hold back on her opinions," I say.

Hudson runs his fingers through his hair and then puts his hat back on. "Let's go share the great news. Where is my future sister-in-law?"

"She's out at the cottage, making plans, as Dad has given his approval for her to live there. You and I have to put a gate in a section of the fence."

"Isn't there already a gate along there?" he asks, puzzled.

"Yeah, but this one is closer to the cottage. The other is pretty far away, and when Mirella moves into the cottage, it'll be easier for her to go to Dotty's and back. Dad's given the okay."

"Sounds good. Let's get to work before I decide to drown myself with a couple of beers instead, and let's go sort out our sisters." He gets up and extends his hands. I take them, and he pulls me up effortlessly.

Back up at the homestead, the girls walk on eggshells around Hudson. Odette, on the other hand, is dancing circles around everyone. At least she's breaking the ice.

Finally, Hudson says, "You can all stop cowering away and thinking I'm going to have a breakdown. Yes, I've got some things to work through, but please don't treat me as though I'm fragile."

"We are sorry about all of this," Mabel says and moves in to give Hudson a hug.

Sybil and Tally follow her.

"Y'all have nothing to be sorry about. I'm not a hundred percent okay, but it's something I'm going to figure out, after some thought and time." Hudson crosses his arms over his broad chest.

Tally places her hand on his arm. "We're all here for you."

"Thanks. Now, I want to set the record straight. Mirella has done nothing wrong, so get over it if you're holding something against her. Well, you need to get over it because she's going to become our next sister-in-law," Hudson announces so loudly I'm sure the people in the cabins and barns hear it.

The room fills with gasps. At that moment, Delilah and Sebastian enter the kitchen. A puzzled look crosses Delilah's face. "What's going on?"

"Harley proposed to Mirella, and she said yes," Sybil squeals and jumps around. She leaps at me and hugs me.

"Another wedding to look forward to," Mabel says, and she almost pushes Sybil aside to get a hug in.

"Oh, double wedding!" Sybil and Mabel scream. The tension that once filled the room has now dissipated. A brand-new energy fills the room right to its corners.

"Whoa, whoa, wait up there. Don't get too excited for that," Delilah calls over the screams from Sybil, Mabel, and Odette. "We haven't decided on anything yet. We aren't rushing into anything at the moment. We're happy as we are." She elbows Sebastian in the ribs.

He expels a puff of air before saying, "What Delilah said. Though, a double wedding does sound good." He winks. The girls get all chatty and excited again. Delilah simply rolls her eyes.

"We can discuss this later. For all we know, Harley and Mirella may not want to share their date, if they have picked one," Mirella says.

"Nope, no date. The question was only asked today. So, give us time to get ourselves settled," I say.

Everyone heads back to their daily jobs that need to be carried out before nighttime. I head back up to my room and spot Mom's letter on my bed where I chucked it this morning. I should be more excited to read something from her, but for the pain she's caused today, I'm angry with her. She kept silent all of Hudson's life. Even Dad being a part of the deception hurts, and it's not even me it pertains to.

I rip the envelope open and see the handwriting I know so well.

Dearest Harley,

You are growing up to be a fine man. I am saddened that I will not get to see you find the perfect young woman to settle down with.

I've kept all these letters short. I want you to know that I love you with all my heart. All of you kids are your father's and my world.

My life has been so blessed, first with your dad, and then your siblings and yourself. I'm sure you're aware of the truth by now with regards to Hudson. Your father is his dad. He raised him, he loved him, and he taught him everything his own father taught him and more. Nothing was ever brought up about his biological father, and he never looked at Hudson as anything other than a son.

Don't think ill of your father or me, please. I know we should have told you all sooner. We didn't want to cause an upset in the home, especially after I'd received the news of my illness and with the care we needed for Odette and the running of the ranch.

Don't ever doubt that I love you with all my heart, though I may not be there now to say those words. Know that I do and remember it.

With love,

Mom

I drop down on the edge of my bed. Tears stream down my face. It's as though I can hear Mom's voice reading those words to me. Closing my eyes, I feel it—her words, her love. She never would intentionally hurt her family. "Oh, Mom, everything is a mess, and I hope it can be cleaned up and things can go back to normal," I whisper to the walls of my empty bedroom. I hope this doesn't ruin my family.

Sure, Hudson is putting on a brave face right now. But I know him. If it were me, it would be tearing me up inside. I will be here for him when the time comes, and he needs my support. He's my only brother, after all.

Chapter 32

Mirella

A week later...

"So, HAVE YOU AND HARLEY decided on the date for your wedding?" Delilah asks as we wade in the shallow part of a beautiful clear creek. Ruby, Olive, and Rylee splash around us and play up on the bank. We watch them play happily. One day, Harley's and my children will be here with their cousins. The thought almost brings tears to my eyes.

"No, not yet. I think it's all still sinking in. How about you and Sebastian? Do you have a date yet?" I drizzle some water over my knees that poke through the water's surface. "Your sisters, Mabel and Sybil, seem to have their hearts set on a double wedding."

Delilah laughs. "I know. They have been harping on about it since Harley proposed. I don't mind the idea," she muses.

"I know what you mean. We could both save a lot of time by doing it together. It's not done often, and it would be cool." The idea of a double wedding makes me excited. I like that thought of sharing the day with someone like Delilah, who is close with Harley.

"Let's think on it and see what our other halves want. Sebastian heads back to the track in the next couple of days. It's going to be a busy time until the end of the Formula One season. I probably won't get anything solid out of him until then."

"I understand," I reply. In that moment, Harley splashes over from across the creek and drops himself down beside me, soaking me a little more. He is a big child, especially when playing with the girls.

"What's going on over here? Talking weddings?" he asks while splashing Rylee. She screams and runs away, then dashes back and splashes him quickly before retreating once again. It's their new game.

"If you must know, we are," Delilah answers with a smile.

Glancing over my shoulder, I catch Hudson sitting on his own against a tree trunk. He's been putting on a brave face, but I can see it in his eyes—the pain and turmoil he's struggling with. There hasn't been any kind of blow-up yet. I have a feeling it might be coming, though. He hasn't spoken about what happened with anyone, and things have been icy between William and him. Hudson is good at putting on a fake smile, but it will only last for so long. I'm worried what might happen when he snaps. A bitter heart and sharp tongue can cause a lot of pain.

"Mirella?" Harley's voice pulls me back into the conversation.

"Sorry, what were you saying?"

"I asked you if you wanted to wait to get married, or would you like sooner rather than later?" He winks.

I think on his question for a moment then say. "I think sooner rather than later. I'm not after a big, lavish wedding, and I only have a handful of friends I'd want to invite." I shrug.

"I like your style, beautiful." He leans forward and presses his lips to my forehead.

"That sounds like me, too. Something small but still beautiful," Delilah muses. "Well, it's something we can talk about later. Let's get some meat cooking." Delilah rises from her spot, water dripping from her. "Sybil and Mabel, would you mind helping me with prepping the food please?" she calls.

Harley is silent beside me, but he reaches over and takes my hand. I take in the scene before me, and this right here has been what I've needed my entire life. A bigger family connection. A love that I didn't know existed. Every family has their issues. Problems don't start or end with my own family, and I'm so glad that my parents and I sorted things out. Mom has called me every day, asking for a date for the wedding. She wants to take me shopping for the occasion to pick out a dress. My problem is going to be getting her to tone the whole wedding down. But I am her only daughter and child, after all. This is what they had originally planned.

William sits on the opposite side of the creek, monitoring Odette and her boyfriend, Devon, who are swinging from a rope into the deep water. The girls play around Harley and me while Delilah, Sybil, and Mabel prep things for our late-afternoon dinner and family time. My eyes shift to Hudson, who hasn't moved, but Tally now sits beside him, and they appear to be having a deep conversation about something. Tally still isn't happy with me, but I think that's just her. I don't know how anyone can carry that much anger around with them. How is anyone supposed to find joy within that unhappiness?

"What are you thinking?" Harley nudges me with his shoulder. My focus turns to him.

"Um, I was thinking about this entire scene. I never have relaxing moments like this with my family. I hope, moving forward, Mom and Dad try to come here more and just relax, not try and talk business and suggest all the things to William." I chuckle. "I didn't realize this was what I'd needed in my life until now. I can't wait to marry you."

"I can't wait either. Mirella, you have been a breath of fresh air around here and within my family. Yeah, things haven't been great with the whole Hudson thing, but we're still a family, and I can't wait for you to be a part of it officially." He comes forward and quickly kisses me and pulls back. "I figure I better tone it down around the family." He laughs.

"I also wanted to say that you need to keep an eye on Hudson. He doesn't seem himself," I say.

Harley nods. "I know. I'm watching him." He turns and glances in Hudson's direction. "We're all keeping an eye on him."

A peaceful stillness settles around us. I have found the man of my dreams, the love of my life, and I am so deliriously happy and excited for what our future holds. Harley is my life. He breathes happiness and joy into me. But for now, I want to live my life with peace and love.

Epilogue

Mirella

Six months later...

"OH, MY GOODNESS, WHERE ARE the bouquets?" Delilah stresses as she moves around the room in her slim-fitting, lace-covered, cream-colored wedding dress. She is beautiful with her blonde hair braided to one side with small yellow flowers placed through it.

"Will you stop stressing like that? You're stressing me out." I take a deep breath and attempt to sit down in my full, fluffy princess gown. My mother said I needed to go all out, so I did this to make her happy, but I also love how this particular dress makes me feel. It has a full tulle skirt with a strapless top. Thank goodness for spray tans because my tan line from working in the sun most days has become pretty bad, and I didn't take that into account when picking this dress.

"You need to get up. You'll crease your dress," Casey chimes as she yanks me from my spot. She is loving it on the ranch. If anything, it'll be getting her to leave that's the problem. But she is a city girl through and through. I'll give it time, and I'll have her staying here more.

I sigh. "Cass, I need to just take five. We've been up since five a.m., finishing off the final touches for the reception." We have a massive white marquee set up along the driveway where we had all the stalls set up for the fundraising fair six months ago.

"Yeah, yeah, it's almost time." Casey flits around the room in her blush-pink halter dress, which has a huge split in it that shows quite a bit of leg.

Sybil, Tally, Delilah, and Odette wear the same color but all in different styles. Delilah and I wanted them to all feel comfortable. Casey is my maid of honor, and Mabel is Delilah's.

Since chatting at the creek that day, Delilah and I have basically planned everything for the wedding together. Thankfully, we both have similar tastes and wanted it very country style with immediate family and close friends in attendance. I didn't want or need something big. My mother had to be reined in quite a few times and roused on for trying to take over. She didn't like it but has finally accepted that this is who I am.

Tally comes to Delilah and me, who stand side by side. The photographer we've hired is snapping away happily, catching our special day. "The fathers are ready to give their daughters away. They are waiting up by the entrance to the ceremony."

Delilah and I look between each other and smile. The butterflies in my stomach swarm. It's finally happening. After months and months of planning, the day has finally arrived.

"Let's get this show on the road. All you girls go first, and we'll follow, just like we practiced," Delilah announces. We're riding side saddle on the horses to the ceremony, which will be held to the side of where the reception is.

We go outside and all mount our horses. Nothing, not even a dress is stopping me from riding Princess to meet my future husband. It took longer than expected, but I finally picked a name for the horse we were training together, and she is the kindest and sweetest girl. So, Princess it is.

Delilah is riding Black Beauty. Dotty wouldn't have it any other way. The relationship between Dotty and William is great. There are still a few kinks in it, but most of the kids have welcomed Dotty. Tally still seems unsure of her, but maybe Dotty can get through to her when the rest of us can't seem to.

"Are you ready?" Delilah calls to all of us. We're almost all on horseback, even Casey, and she's, surprisingly, a natural. Odette is on Butter, of course. Tally won't have anything to do with horses and has chosen to walk ahead and wait for us. I know how she feels, but I'm glad I'm on one now.

"Let's do this," Sybil says and starts walking. She's holding an extra rein for Butter, since Odette is riding her. Delilah and I glance at each other.

"I guess this is what we have been preparing for. Let's go marry the loves of our lives," Delilah says with a small nudge to Black Beauty's tummy. I do the same, and Princess follows nicely.

As we come over the small hill of the driveway, Harley comes into view. He's dressed in black jeans and a white shirt. His shiny belt buckle glitters under the sun, and his cowboy hat sits nicely on his head. He is the man of my dreams, and I can't wait to be his wife — and tell him we're expecting a baby.

Delilah and I climb down from the horses. The girls have walked down the aisle, and now it's our turn. William holds out his arm for Delilah to take, which she does, and he walks her down the aisle to a waiting Sebastian, who has tears in his eyes. Dad steps in beside me. I take his arm, and it's my turn to walk down the aisle. I clutch a small bouquet of wildflowers Odette has picked for me this morning. She also gathered a bouquet for Delilah. Mine has the positive pregnancy test I took this morning inside it.

Our baby wasn't planned at all, but these things can happen when you're too caught up in the moment and don't protect yourself. I giggle at the thought. I glance over at Mom, who has tears in her eyes. I haven't told anyone yet about the baby.

Hudson claps Harley on the back. Gosh, meeting Harley and thinking about what we went through, what his family has gone through, and what Hudson is still dealing with... I'm so happy we're here in this moment. Dad hands me over to Harley. They shake hands, and Dad sits down.

"You look beautiful," Harley whispers.

"You look handsome." I grin. Before I hand off my flowers to Rylee, who waits patiently to one side, I take the test out of it. I hand the flowers to her and then hand the test to Harley.

It takes him a moment, then his head shoots up, and our eyes connect. Tears are in his, and they well in mine, too, but I blink them away because of my makeup. "You're going to be a daddy," I whisper.

He leaps forward, scooping me up in his arms. "Hey, we're not ready for that yet," Delilah says from beside us.

"I'm going to be a dad!" Harley announces to everyone and plants a kiss on my mouth as the guests applaud.

"I'm going to be a mom again!" Delilah announces, and there's another loud applause from our guests. I hug Delilah and Sebastian, as does Harley.

To know my kid is going to grow up and be close to their cousins and bring me so much joy. "I love you," I say to Harley as we compose ourselves again.

"I love you, too. You've made me the happiest man today."

"And you've made me the happiest woman. Now, let's make this official."

The End

Thank you so much for reading Harley and Mirella's story.

Want Hudson's story?
Sign up at subscribepage.com/roseridgeranch

Turn the page for a look at
Something Old (The Jilted Series, #1)

Grab your copy - books2read.com/u/mlW8oW

And come join my reader group **Lovelock's Flock**
facebook.com/groups/742675105787263

Preview
Something Old

Chapter One
Scarlett

How did my life end up like this?

For the second time in my short thirty years, I'm sitting in a divorce attorney's office.

"Did you hear me?"

My attention clicks to my soon-to-be, second, ex-husband, Craig. The smug grin on his face makes my hand twitchy. Loving him used to be so easy… but it turned into something sour.

"No, I didn't, sorry." I attempt to keep my voice even.

He huffs and rolls his eyes. "That's your problem, Scarlett, and why we're here. You never were present. Your work always took *first* priority. Not me."

My back straightens as I lay my hands flat on the table. I shut my eyes briefly and open them again, staring directly at Craig. "Excuse me! That *work* you speak of gave you the life you've enjoyed living for the past two years, and don't even get me started on your lazy ass."

Vivian lays her perfectly manicured hand on my arm. I snap my mouth shut and bite the inside of my bottom lip. I inhale a large breath through my nose and then release it, hoping to expel the bubbling anger rising in me. My body vibrates. How I put up with this man has me baffled. What the ever-loving hell did I see in him?

Vivian clears her throat and tosses her blonde hair over her shoulder. I hang my head and train my focus on my hands as they rest on the dark-wood conference room table. If I have to talk again, I might not be able to rein in the verbal abuse that threatens to spew from my mouth.

"My client has informed me that she has been the income provider in this marriage." Vivian pauses a moment, and I glance up at her. She winks then continues. "Thankfully, my client listens to her lawyer, and when she was told to get a prenup signed, she did."

I don't miss the smugness emanating from her words. He's paled significantly.

Craig quickly leans into his lawyer and whispers something.

"My client has no recollection of signing a prenup," his lawyer states matter-of-factly.

I shoot a worried glance in Vivian's direction. The soft look of reassurance in her green eyes tells me she has what she needs.

Vivian lifts some paperwork from her file and slides it across the table. "This is a copy that *obviously* has his signature on it. Does he have short-term memory loss? There are even witnesses to the signing, me being one of them." She stops, and a look of confidence passes from her to me. The weight that's been sitting on my chest lifts slightly. Thankfully, I listened to her on this when she shoved paperwork in my face.

I'd thought Craig was different. Most guys who date me don't know that I come from money. Craig, though, is the son of one of my father's business partners.

When we met, he was this sweet, caring guy. We were married within six months. Our families were over the moon, and I was, too— until I noticed the things he'd buy with my money. From there, things went downhill at a fast pace.

He played me.

His lawyer collects and scans the document, and he and Craig speak in quiet whispers.

"Do you think things will go smoothly?" I whisper to Vivian, who's busy shuffling papers around.

She side-eyes me. "Honey, you should have listened to me long ago." Her words sting, but they're true. She warned me. My best friend sighs and faces me. "I've got you. We made sure this prenup could not be bent. Even if he bought things, if he used your money, then it's yours. You own everything, and he has nothing. Anything that's in his name is all he gets, plus whatever he came into the marriage with, which, from memory, wasn't much at all."

I wish I had her confidence. "I'm glad you're on my side," I mutter.

"I always will be."

After a moment, Craig's lawyer clears his throat. "My client wants the apartment in New York."

My attention shifts to him, and I want to vomit. That's my favorite place, and Craig knows it.

"No," Vivian shoots back sternly before I can even protest. Judging by the vein pulsing at her throat, she may not have been expecting this. Neither was I.

"We're not negotiating. He leaves with everything he came into the marriage with. Here's a list of all that my client will be keeping. Your client can have the same apartment he had when they first got married. I believe his father bought it for him." She slides a single sheet of paper across the table to him.

"But…" Craig jumps up from his seat. His face is flaming red, and heavy breaths push from his mouth. "I'm *owed* something." It almost sounds like a growl.

His eyes burn into Vivian's.

Her expression is blank and devoid of emotion, very professional. "Craig, you've been married for eighteen months and together for two years in total. All properties are in my client's name, and she owned them before you came into her life. What makes you think you are owed anything? She has worked hard for what she has, but according to my records, you haven't been working for the past six months. You've been living off her hard work since then."

"It's not my fault she's a workaholic and couldn't be bothered with her marriage," he mutters before sitting back down.

"So, me working meant it was okay for you to sleep with someone else? Did she make you feel better? And if you had read the whole document before you signed it, you'd know it states that if you cheat, you get nothing except what you came into the marriage with. Don't give me your sob story, Craig. You made your bed—now you have to sleep in it. Can we finish this up now?" The words rush from me, my chest tight.

Vivian twists in my direction. Her mouth hangs open, and her eyes are wide. "I thought we weren't going to use that against him."

"I was trying to let him keep some dignity. I guess that's out the window now," I whisper.

"How did—" Craig stares at me.

"You may think I had my face buried in my work, but I noticed the little things. I noticed the nights you were gone, the secret calls and text messages. I'm not blind to what goes on around me." I rest back into my seat.

The room turns stale and silent.

Vivian doesn't take too long to bring all the attention back to what needs to happen. Her in a courtroom is powerful; I think men underestimate her. "Well, this should be wrapped up in a neat little bow from here on out. I suggest we get the paperwork signed and move on with our day." She clicks her pen, rests it on the settlement agreement, and then slides it across the table. The winning grin plastered on her face says it all.

I can't wait for this entire charade to be over. Perhaps I'm destined to become a cat woman. Being alone may not be such a bad thing; it's something I could get accustomed to. My father wasn't around much, and Mom kept herself busy, and I seem to marry and divorce any guy that catches my attention. I've learned my lesson now. No more guys—just work.

By the end of the meeting, I walk out with everything still intact—all the belongings I had at the start of our marriage, thanks to Vivian's wise advice. I'd hate to see my publishing business destroyed. It's something that's mine and mine alone.

"Well, that's it, then. Please don't marry anyone else for the time being." Vivian struts beside me, her black, shiny heels clicking on the marbled floor as we exit the building.

I laugh and playfully shove her shoulder. "Thanks for everything."

The lump in my throat thickens; no one wants to admit their husband has been unfaithful.

Vivian's arm wraps around my shoulders. "I'm here for you. Let's grab some lunch and have a cocktail or two. What do you say?"

"No thanks. I'm just going back to the office and drowning myself in work."

She stops and faces me, the worry lines in her forehead more predominant. Her hands go to her hips. "Don't do that. Don't shut yourself away." *Now comes the lecture.* She crosses her arms over her navy-blue satin top, her cream pencil skirt complimenting it well.

The lasso wrapped around my chest tightens. "I just want to be alone right now. Maybe we can catch up later this week."

Vivian agrees, and we say our goodbyes. I head in the direction of my office a couple of blocks away. It's my safe place. The one thing that keeps me grounded and happy.

I can't believe how my life has turned out. I've messed things up.

The only sound I hear is my high heels clicking on the sidewalk, and I scan all the faces around me. People-watching is something I enjoy. A woman with a baby—perhaps it's a secret baby, and the father doesn't even know the cutie in the pram is alive, but, thanks to fate, when they run into each other at her friend's wedding, love blooms.

Warmth blossoms in my chest. Who doesn't love a good love story? Like the ones in the romance books I publish.

A horn blares behind me. I jump, my heart skipping a couple of beats. I stop and face the road, cars, businessmen, beautiful women.

Across the street, a tall, blond man catches my attention. Squinting, I try to make out his face. It couldn't be. *Is it Lachlan?* No, my mind is playing tricks on me. There are plenty of blond men around. *What would be the odds of me running into my first ex-husband the day I divorced the second?*

My head must be taunting me with past mistakes. That's all I seem to be good at. Bad choices. Poor judgment. Stupid mistakes.

Grab your copy of
Something Old (The Jilted series, #1) at
books2read.com/u/mlVV8oVV.

Other Books by Liz Lovelock

Lost Series

The Lost One — Book One

The Missing One — Book Two

Lost Series Boxed Set

Letters in Blood Series

Dear Captor — Book One

With Love — Book Two

Forever Yours — Book Three

Dear Captor Boxed Set

My Guy Series

Monday Night Guy — Book One

My Aussie Guy — Book Two

My Forbidden Guy — Book Three

The Right Guy — Book Four

My Guy Series Complete Boxed Set

Other Books by Liz Lovelock

The Jilted Series

Something Old — Book One

Something New — Book Two

Something Borrowed — Book Three

Something Blue — Book Four

Something Beautiful — Book Five — A Novella

Rose Ridge Ranch Series

The One to Heal — Book One

The One to Protect — Book Two

Acknowledgements

I'll say sorry first in case I miss anyone. The One to Protect was such an amazing story to write. I love these characters and love what their future books will be like.

I'd like to thank all those who helped get The One to Heal in tip top shape—Lauren from Creating Ink, Lisa Vincent and Jenn Lockwood Editing. Without you ladies, I'd be thoroughly lost. You've all pushed me with this one. You're awesome! Thanks for all your advice and guidance.

A huge thank you to Ben from Tall Story for designing the perfect cover. It is everything I wanted it to be. I love it!

These next mentions are my other halves in the author world. Without their constant support and friendship, I may have given up a long time ago. They're my cyber sisters spread far and wide around Australia and America, so thank you to Jemma Brown aka JB Heller, Donna, and Belle Brooks. These ladies are truly amazing. I'd be lost without our chats.

Huge shout out to my awesome Beta Readers who offered heaps of support and encouragement. Thank you Donna, Anastasia, Halle, Margaret, Sheena, Tracey and Vicki.

To my Flock—I love you, girls. Your support is truly nothing short of amazing. I know I have a safe place in my group with you all. Thank you.

To my readers—I feel blessed to have your continuous support. Thank you.

To my family and my husband—you're truly wonderful. You've never given up on me. You sit and listen when I need to vent out my frustrations, never once complaining about it. I love you.

To my three beautiful children—Millie, Cale, and Finn. You three test my patience, but I'm so grateful to have you in my life to love. Families are forever.

About the Author

I'm a wife, mother, reader, blogger, and now an author. I'm always busy doing something as I have so much going on, and my three little ones keep me on my toes.

I'm from bright and sunny Queensland, Australia. I have always been a reader. When I was little, I would be up late reading *Garfield* and *Asterix* comic books and also *Footrot Flats*. When I hit high school, they gave us *Tomorrow When the War Began* by John Marsden, and from there my love of books continued to grow.

I keep a notebook and pen beside my bed for when those late-night ideas pop into my head, plus I'm a stationery addict and love pens, notebooks, and, well, anything stationery.

Connect with Liz Online

Check these links for more information about author Liz Lovelock.

TikTok ~ tiktok.com/@lizlovelockauthor

Email ~ lizlovelockauthor@gmail.com

Website ~ lizlovelockauthor.com/

Facebook ~ facebook.com/people/Liz-Lovelock-Author/100008389321975/

Goodreads ~ goodreads.com/author/show/8268717.Liz_Lovelock

Instagram ~ instagram.com/lizlovelock/

Or sign up for my **Newsletter**:
app.mailerlite.com/webforms/landing/w4c9g7

www.ingramcontent.com/pod-product-compliance
Lightning Source LLC
Chambersburg PA
CBHW020346120726
47904CB00002B/473